Friends to the End
by
Trudy W. Schuett

Friends to the End

Trudy W. Schuett

Friends to the End

©2008 by Trudy W. Schuett

Library of Congress Control Number: 2007909947
ISBN 978-0-6151-9073-0

As this is a work of fiction, the names, people, and their actions are used fictitiously. Nothing in this book is intended to slander or misrepresent any individual or group.

First Lulu edition – February 2008

Please contact DAHMW for bulk orders.
http://www.dahmw.com
1-888-7-HELPLINE

Friends to the End

A Note from the Author

When I began writing this book nearly eight years ago, I had no idea that the simple idea of writing a novel with an evil woman as part of the story would change my life.

Yet it has, and in ways I never expected.

Like most people, I had the mistaken idea that since everything else was now equal, the services for battered women I heard so much about would be complemented by services for men.

As a product of my research into the realities of domestic violence, when the primary victim is male, I found that even in 1999, decades after domestic violence had become a public concern, there was still no help for men. What's more, existing programs attempted to both blame men for the entire problem and deny the fact of female abusers.

I knew from my own life experience that this is not a gender issue. In fact, the first violently abusive person I met was a woman; the mother of a friend from elementary school. I heard of other violent women along the way, and at least one male victim who was forced to leave his children and home behind, simply to stay alive.

I was outraged that the issue had been so distorted and wrongfully approached; in a way that could be of little or no possible help to anyone, save those opportunistic individuals who were more interested in personal gain and revenge-seeking against their own personal devils. The politicization of domestic violence, which is a purely human problem requiring human solutions, represents in my mind, one of the lowest points of American history.

How we can, as a society, sit idly by while people in misery are subjected to bigotry and punishment simply for being victims, is not something I have ever understood.

There are a few bright spots for victims of domestic violence, however. The general acceptance of the bill of goods originally sold the American people by snake oil salesgirls has begun to be seriously questioned, and bit by bit, the truth is emerging.

The Domestic Abuse Helpline for Men & Women has been instrumental in shedding light on this hidden subject, and is for that reason I'm donating all proceeds from this book to that excellent agency. Originally begun in 2000 as the Battered Men's Helpline, it changed to DAHMW because of the extremely narrow demographic served by other agencies, and now has become the only nationwide agency providing equal services to all, regardless of gender.

Domestic Abuse Helpline for Men & Women
888-7-HELPLINE
http://www.dahmw.org/

ACKNOWLEDGEMENTS

First and foremost, I'd like to thank my husband Paul, for his patience and perseverance in living with a writer; and my son, Sean, for being proud of his mom and giving me brilliant advice along the way.

Doreen Conti; my daughter-in-law, who has not forgotten how families work when men are involved. I thank God everyday she has come into our lives.

I can't do this kind of thanks exercise without remembering my dear friend, Richard Hayden, who founded the Abused Guys Group, and who is sadly, no longer with us, and Karl Glasson, of Angry Harry fame. They were my first cheerleaders and supporters in this long journey into hard copy. Richard said when he read an early copy, "Everybody needs to read this book!"

Dr. Charles Corry and Raymond Cuttill provided important lessons.

Steven DeLuca, who always reminds me there are people out there who need us to reach them.

Dean Esmay, who gave me a larger podium.

Jan Brown, who has been invaluable in so many ways.

Harry Crouch, for providing a stellar example.

Paul Whitlock, my brother, who never thought I shouldn't write.

Ernestine Colvin – my late, but much-loved aunt, who inexplicably once told me "Real people don't write books."

We Cannot Forget

The thousands of men who are abused and killed each year; not to forget their children also at risk. I pray this book will serve as a reminder that there is someone out there who cares; who understands we should begin to focus on the problem itself, and its many origins and causes, rather than the people afflicted by it.

Trudy W. Schuett

Chapter One

The phone had been quiet for days, and the ringing startled Mary as she shut down the computer for the weekend. She reached over and picked it up, after she found it under a week's worth of unread mail.

It was Donna, her next-door neighbor. "Hey, Mare, think we want to try the pool party today?"

The apartment complex where they lived gave twice-monthly parties for the residents, to make up for the lack of things like individual washers and dryers, and work-out rooms that newer complexes had.

"Why not? Carla across the hall from you said they're great, but it's mainly older people and you know what she means..."

"Yeah, everybody's over 30—we should fit right in. You mean I can actually pry you out of that computer chair?"

"Sure, it's the weekend. I recognize these things now Eliot's gone," Mary chuckled. "There is life out there, and not everybody's a jaded 'puter geek, even in Seattle."

"Even a jaded 'puter geek would look good to me now! Sheesh! You know it's been two years since my divorce and I haven't had a real date in months and months?"

"Yes, I do know that. It's your mantra, almost—"

"Well, at least you've got the excuse that you work 24 hours a day. What's that about, I'd like to know."

"The e-publishing world would grind to a halt without me? Uh, I don't know--"

There was a knock on the door. Donna, with her phone in her hand. She hung it up, and said; as she tossed the phone back into her apartment through the open door, "Don't know why we bother to phone each other. What do you think of this suit?" She was wearing a bright red, two-piece bathing suit, that would have looked terrible if she had two ounces of extra fat where it shouldn't be. She was tall enough, and slim enough, to carry it off.

"That is great! Wish I was brave enough to wear something like that. If I had any boobs, I might."

"You do, but nobody'd ever know it in those Victorian—" Donna was interrupted by a door opening across the hall.

"Hey, guys, you goin' to the pool party? Steve's got lotsa beer, and we've got extra chairs." Carla came down the hall wearing a yellow sundress.

"Not going in?" Donna asked.

"Uh-uh." Carla shook her head. "That's just too much water all in one place."

The apartment complex had an Olympic-sized pool, the result of a former owner's conviction that one day the Olympics had to come to Seattle. The Olympics never happened, but the pool was an amenity for some.

"Guess what? There's a new guy over there—" Carla pointed to the apartment across the hall from Mary. "Just moved in yesterday. Steve talked to him, and he's like, 28 or something. He was out swimming at six o'clock in the morning! God! Steve said he was out there for like an hour just going back and forth, and back and forth."

"A dedicated swimmer, huh?" Mary looked at Donna and shrugged. "A jock?" Mary was not into sports. She had been to the occasional football game when she was going to the University of Michigan, when she couldn't get out of it, but she always took a paperback book along to keep from getting bored.

"Sounds just fine to me!" Donna grinned. "He's breathing, he's ambulatory—that's all I care about! "

"A little young for me," Mary said.

"Oh, you're getting picky, huh? You're only 33, it's not like you're 43, for god's sake." Donna said.

"Actually, I'm being gracious—a 28-year-old jock sounds more your type."

"Nope, you're being normal," Carla, said. "You wouldn't go out with any of our friends!"

"Your friends acquainted me with the meaning of the term, 'jailbait'," Mary laughed. "Half of them aren't even out of high school!"

Steve and Carla had taken Mary under their wings after her fiancé, Eliot left her to live with his friend, Lynn. They felt sorry for her, moving all the way out here from Detroit, only to be dumped a week before the wedding.

"You gotta admit they're fun, though," Donna said, looking at Mary and winking. "I don't have your scruples anymore. Wait till you've been alone as long as I have, your standards will change!"

"God, I'm glad I'm married. I wouldn't want to date now for anything! I'll catch you guys later, huh?" Carla went back to her own apartment. As she opened her door, she turned and said, "Wait till you see him!"

Hours later, Mary got out of the pool and was toweling off, when Donna said, "I think I just died and went to heaven." She was lying on a chaise lounge with her big hat over her eyes. Mary knew she could see right through it.

Carla said, "That's him! Don't know who the other one is. If I wasn't married, I'd be over there in a heartbeat. Talk about gorgeous!" Carla was in her twenties and happily married to Steve since high school.

Mary had her back to the pool.

"They're looking at you, Mary." Donna said. "Both of them. That guy in the green's lookin' at your butt. Oh-my-God! I don't think I've ever seen two guys that hot together in one place before."

Carla said, "I wonder if they're twins?"

"Now I gotta sit down and be cool, huh? And why today, of all days, I ask you? I should've worn a freaking muumuu! I feel like an elephant with all this water retention." Mary pulled her cover-up off the back of the chair and put it on. "Are they still looking at me?"

"No, looks like one of them is leaving. Wanna arm wrestle for the other one, Mare?" Donna said. "Wonder if they're both jocks."

Mary ignored that. "At least I can sit down now. Where's my sunglasses?"

As Mary was sitting down, looking for her sunglasses in the grass, Carla said, "I'm goin' for beers, anybody want one? How about you?"

A deep male voice answered, "Sure, why not?"

Mary looked up, and there was Keith.

Not the guy in the green who'd been looking at her butt. Not that she'd seen either one. It was true, though, Keith was hot. There was something else there, too. There was no eyes-glazed-over, politeness- while- looking- for- an- escape reaction she often got after she told guys what she did for a living. She saw a spark of interest when she said she was a publisher.

Carla and Donna nudged each other, looking on in amazement as Mary and Keith both let their beers get warm and talked like long-lost friends. Later, it started to look like rain, and they all went in to Steve and Carla's to play "Trivial Pursuit". Either Keith or Mary won every round, and it wasn't till after that Keith admitted to being an English teacher. This, of course, gave him and Mary even more to talk about.

Steve and Carla congratulated themselves on finding "Heartbroken Mary" a guy, after they'd said goodnight to everybody. But they were wrong.

That night, Mary lay in her bed, tired, but not ready for sleep. Tonight's party was more fun than she had in a long, long time.

Mary knew because of their age difference, and the fact of Keith's stunning, dark good looks, they would probably be never more than buddies. Neighbors. He was a big man, with wide shoulders and powerful arms from many years of swimming every day. He had a million-candlepower smile and eyes that reminded her of that welcome first hot cup of coffee in the morning. But he seemed to understand her, and actually paid attention when she was talking, a big change from Eliot's distraction. Mary thought she was plain, even unattractive—she had so far only had boyfriends that were too preoccupied to notice a beautiful, sensuous woman when they saw one.

Keith was wondering about Mary in his own place across the hall. She made it clear from the very beginning her plans didn't include him. He thought she was really looking for a computer guy with zillions of dollars, a summer house in Maui and a flat in London. But she had a dark beauty with a quality of something deep and wonderful behind those green cat's eyes. She was a tiny thing, but with so much energy and intelligence he wondered where she put it all. It seemed he could ask her about anything, and she would always have an answer.

The next week, Keith had an afternoon barbecue as a housewarming party and invited his brothers Kevin and Kirk, and Kirk's wife Vickie. He also invited his new neighbors. Kevin and Donna hit it off right away, which made Mary feel better about monopolizing Keith the week before. Carla and Steve were impressed by Vickie, because she was a cop. Carla said she looked more like a woman executive for a corporation or something. Vickie was almost as tall as her husband, and as a natural blonde had worked hard to dispel the 'dumb blonde' image. She had succeeded well. Mary liked her straightforward manner of speaking, without the 'tough broad' manner so many female police officers seemed to project.

Kirk was every bit as great-looking as his brothers, even though he was 38. In the kitchen getting more beers to take outside, Donna said to Mary, "Maybe they improve with age, ya think? Can you imagine? Kevin said the oldest one is 48. Wow!"

Mary only laughed. Keith was way out of her league, but he was good to talk to, anyway.

It was one of those low-key, friendly kinds of parties. Nobody had too much to drink; there was plenty of conversation going on all the time. Kevin and Donna kept disappearing, and eventually they left altogether. There wasn't that kind of chemistry going on with Keith and Mary.

Sunday morning Mary was struggling with her laundry basket, full of clothes and bottles of soap and bleach, trying to get the door of the laundry room open without dropping anything.

"Let me get that door," Keith said, appearing out of nowhere. He reached over her head and pushed the door open, shifting his laundry basket to one arm. "You always do laundry on Sunday, or do you wait until there's absolutely nothing left to wear?"

"I do Sundays, mainly. As early as possible, because you can't get near the place later. I could do it anytime, really, but I can't seem to get out of the habit of working Monday through Friday."

"It must take a lot of discipline to work at home." He remarked, dumping his whole basket of laundry in one machine. *Typical guy*, Mary noted.

"I did a lot of freelance writing when I lived in Detroit, so I'm used to it. But I guess you know about discipline, out there in the pool at six every morning," she said as she carefully sorted her clothes into three machines. Usually if there was a guy in the laundry room, she hoped he wasn't paying attention to her underwear. This time she forgot to think about it.

"You have to do something to keep in shape—swimming's something you can do without needing a team. My brothers all played basketball in college, and now they're all pretty much going to pot, except for Phil, because he works outside all the time."

He thought Kevin and Kirk were going to pot? Well, now... "What does Phil do?"

"He works for the Central Arizona Project. He spends a lot of time in a four-wheel-drive out in the desert looking at pipelines and whatnot. A lot of walking and climbing over rocks. He's the eldest, by the way. The next eldest, Brian, owns a technical school in Phoenix. He pretty much sits behind a desk all day."

"And they're all big, tall, guys like you and Kevin, and, um—"

"Kirk, yeah. Actually, I'm the shortest, don't know if you noticed from down there." He grinned. "My mom's a shortie like you, though. Hey, I've got pictures of everybody up on the wall now, let's go over and you can see."

Mary put quarters in the last machine, and turned around. "Sure. I hate sitting here doing nothing."

In a few hours, the laundry room and the pool would be crowded, but now they were the only people outside. The three, four-story buildings sat in a "U" shape around the pool, with the laundry room in a smaller building at one end with the manager's office and community room. They crossed the grass and went to Keith's by the back door facing the pool. Inside, the apartment was so neat no one would ever think there had been a dozen people here the day before. Though it was exactly the same size inside as Mary's, this apartment felt bigger because of the glass patio door.

On the wall over the couch, Mary counted 25 framed pictures—all of the Astor family. Some of them may have been as much as a hundred years old, but the family resemblance was strong in all of them. One showed Keith and his four brothers standing around their parents, who were sitting down. "That one was taken the day before the birthday party last year. Every three or four years, my parents get one done. But see what I mean?" Keith said.

"Gosh, how tall is Phil?" Mary was surprised at how much taller than Keith he was. Bigger in every way, it seemed.

"Oh, I think about six foot five. Close to three hundred pounds, too. I'm only about 215. Mom's sitting down, huh? Well, let's see...oh, here." He pointed to a small snapshot with three tall, queen-sized women and one short, older lady. Mary recognized Vickie on the end.

"That's Bobbie, she's Phil's wife, Brenda, she's Brian's wife, and Vickie you know. But that's mom." He looked carefully back at Mary, his eyes narrowed. "I think you're both about the same height."

"Whose birthday was it?"

"Oh, that, sorry, everybody knows...it's Mom's birthday. They've been having a big party, more like a family reunion, every year since Mom and Dad were first married." He pointed to an older, black and white photo. Three boys and two babies, same parents. "Recognize any of these guys?"

"The babies have to be you and Kevin." Mary resisted saying, "You were such cute babies, too!" Instead she said, "Was it a lot of fun growing up with all those brothers? My parents just had me, and that was enough."

He shrugged. "People ask me that all the time, and it was a lot different than you'd think. By the time I was born, Phil was already in college. Brian was in high school, and he was seriously into basketball in the winter and in the summer, he worked with Dad, so he was hardly ever home. Before he retired, Dad had a construction business. Every one of us spent our summers working for him when we were old enough. So it was Kirk, Kevin and me most of the time—more like having two brothers instead of four."

"I spent almost every summer with my grandma in upstate New York. Dad's a psychologist, and mom used to be a militant feminist. Pretty strange when you think she was married with a baby. But she went to New York one year when they had a demonstration and burned her bra along with everybody else." She shrugged. "I could never quite understand it. They're leftover hippies, really. They went to Woodstock, and they've been all over the world finding themselves."

Keith laughed. "So have they ever? Or do they keep finding different selves?"

"I have no idea." She grinned up at Keith. "'course, they're always finding somebody. They've got an 'open marriage'. When I was a kid, I never knew who I'd find having breakfast with us in the morning."

"My parents aren't like that at all. They're about as close to Ozzie and Harriet as it gets. Mom's social activism was limited to being a scout leader, and I think she was President of the PTA once. Of course by the 60s, they already had Phil and Brian. I don't think my dad ever looked at another woman. No, that's not my parents at all."

Keith went on to explain who the grandparents and great-grandparents were in the older pictures. The Astor family had been in the area since the 30s, when Keith's grandfather came over from Scotland, and had been involved in building or selling houses ever since.

Mary and Keith went back to check on their laundry, and there were now one or two other people in the laundry room. Mary was finished first, and packed up her laundry, heading back to her apartment.

"Why don't you just go thru my place? It's a lot closer that way—the patio door's open," Keith said, as he held the door for her on her way out.

That was the first of many Sundays they did laundry together.

With Kevin and Donna paired off, and Keith and Mary 'just hangin', the first four apartments on the ground floor soon became a summer-long social event. It was more fun to be home than anywhere else, and one morning Mary realized as she looked at the calendar she hadn't gone anywhere but the grocery store in months.

She picked up the phone to suggest to Donna that a night out for all of them might be a good idea. Maybe Keith could suggest a good place to go. She knew Kevin's expensive tastes, and didn't want to embarrass Steve and Carla by suggesting someplace they couldn't afford. The phone rang for a long time before it was picked up.

"Hi, Mare," Donna said. It was clear she'd checked her caller ID. She sounded disappointed. "You're not Kevin."

"No, I guess not. Hey, I thought it would be a good idea for the bunch of us to go out this weekend. I haven't been out of this place in way too long."

"Might be OK, but—I haven't heard from Kev in two weeks. You haven't seen him, have you?"

Uh-oh.

"He doesn't answer his phone, I've even left messages at work. I don't know what to think."

"Did you two have a fight or something?"

"No, nothing. I spent the night at his place, and he had to go to work that Saturday morning—I know that, I've been in real estate long enough to know you can't plan too much. We were going to have dinner here and then see what you guys were up to, but he never showed up. I haven't seen him since." More than being disappointed, Donna was crying now. "He told me he loved me, Mare. Guess I was stupid enough to believe him."

Mary didn't know what to say to poor Donna. Keith hadn't said much about Kevin, beyond the fact that he made more money than anybody else in the family. Mary suspected the similarity between the two men stopped at their appearance. Kevin seemed more interesting in talking about the money he was making and the things he was buying than anything else. Keith seldom talked about money, and seemed far more interested in other people than Kevin did. Kevin seemed to be one of those guys who really wanted a living Barbie doll with a mirror in her hand so he could check his hair every five minutes.

Later that afternoon, Mary intercepted Keith as he was coming home from work. She saw him pulling into the parking lot and was waiting in her open doorway as he came down the hall.

He grinned when he saw her. "Just the person I wanted to see. Have you ever made lasagna? I told Carla I'd make dinner for everybody tonight."

"Ooh, you're brave—Steve's Italian!" she chuckled. "But, yeah, I've made it. Layers, noodles—what do you want to know?"

"Everything."

"Oh, geez—sure, I'll help. It takes a while, we should get going on it soon."

"Well, give me twenty minutes and just come on over, OK?"

This gave her a perfect opportunity to go fishing. As the sauce was simmering, and Keith was grating cheese at the kitchen table, she asked, as casually as possible, "So, have you seen Kevin lately?"

Keith knew exactly what she was asking. "He dumped Donna—am I right?"

She nodded.

"That's Kev for ya. He puts all his energy into a relationship and then wakes up one morning and decides he's bored. And that's it. If it's been more than a week, he's got somebody else already. Did he suddenly have to go to work when they had plans?"

"Yep."

"Well, that's it then. I just hope she wasn't in too deep, Donna's a nice lady." He looked up from the cheese, with a hopeful expression.

"She set up camp by the phone," Mary said, shaking her head. "She says he told her—"

"Yeah, he tells everybody that. He could be the poster boy for fear of commitment. She's going to have to get over him; he doesn't ever go back that I know of. You'd think at his age he'd quit playing these college-level games." He shook his head. "One day he's going to wake up and be 55, totally out of shape, and not so cute anymore, and then where'll he be? But of course, that doesn't do Donna any good right now. I guess all you can do is hold her hand, and hope she doesn't take it too hard."

Donna did take it too hard. So hard, in fact, that within another month she had
moved to San Diego to nurse her broken heart. Mary could understand it would be hard
for her to live in the same complex as Keith, when he looked so much like Kevin, but
wished she didn't need to move quite so far away.

Things got worse when Steve and Carla announced they, too, would be moving, but for happier reasons. Carla was pregnant, and they had bought a house. Keith and Mary were thrilled for them, if a little wistful. Even though he hadn't come out and said so, Mary knew Keith was hoping for marriage and kids as much as she was. No Barbie dolls for Keith—what he deserved was more on the order of Miss America with an IQ of 180, a Cordon Bleu graduate who also held a degree in pediatric nursing.

The Saturday night after their three friends had moved out, Mary and Keith were alone for the first time. It had become almost a routine for both of them to separately wander over to Carla and Steve's at some point on Saturday.

That Saturday, Mary shut down the computer for the day and went out to the pool and paddled around by herself for a while. She was floating on her back in the shallow end, looking up at the sky when Keith appeared. This was dinnertime for most people, and they were alone at the pool.

"That's an excellent imitation of a dead goldfish, was it hard to learn?" Keith said.

"Definitely. Years of practice," she said. She stood up in the water and looked around. "It's really quiet around here with everybody gone, isn't it?"

"Yeah, it is. I went over to Steve and Carla's earlier for a little while. They're having a big housewarming thing, and they invited all their friends. Some of them either have been or were my students, so I didn't hang around long." He sat down on the side of the pool. "Didn't want to put a damper on things. I have a hard time enjoying myself when everybody's calling me Mr. Astor."

"I know how you feel. That's precisely why I had something else pressing I had to do. It was different when Donna was still here, they didn't seem like such kids somehow."

"Have you had your dinner yet? I was thinking about trying to make a pizza, from the ground up."

"You don't know how? I could make pizza in my sleep. Back in Detroit, some nights Eliot would be working late, and I'd make three or four of them and take them over to his office." She grinned ruefully.

"Why did you do that? He couldn't pick up a phone and call the pizza place?" Keith grinned down at her.

"Not that he couldn't—he wouldn't. I didn't realize how cheap he was until after we moved out here. I had looked at it as something to do when I was by myself at night. Then when we moved in together, he'd do stuff like go through the phone bill item by item and he'd e-mail me a bill for my calls."

"E-mail? He couldn't just hand it to you?" Keith was amused by that.

"Heavens, no. He wanted to have a record that I owed him three dollars. Big woo. I don't know what he expected to do after we got married." She got out of the pool and went over to dry off, and Keith followed.

"My ex, Wendy, used to insist on making my lunch every day. She'd make sandwiches on whole wheat bread, and cut them into quarters. I'd get either an orange or a banana, and if it was an orange she'd cut it up. Anything else she'd put in those tiny little plastic containers that hold about two ounces. Then she'd put it all into a brown paper bag, and write my name on it, for chrissakes! I didn't dare lose any of those plastic things either--."

They looked at each other and laughed. "Think we're better off, huh?" Mary said.

"You got that right! The day we broke up, I told her she really wanted to live with Peter Pan."

"I sent Eliot a bill for computer storage— only I Fed Ex'ed it. He probably didn't 'get' the message, but he sure got the bill!"

"Computer storage?"

"Yeah, it was just like living with one, except you know where your computer is at night. So, how about I make the crust, and you do the top?"

That night's pizza was the first of many to follow. It was also the first of many nights they'd spend together, never getting much closer to each other than about two feet. That night was a long, exhaustive debriefing of their former relationships with Wendy and Eliot, with few of their perceived faults left undiscussed. To both Keith and Mary's surprise, they talked all night. There were birds singing in the trees when Mary finally went home the next morning.

Mary was always home. As an electronic publisher, her office was in her living room and she was making tons of money and working hard. One day she expected to buy a house, and maybe find some time to date or meet some men her own age. Her life could really take off then, but meanwhile she was content to spend her small amount of downtime with Keith. He even went shopping with her to help her pick out a big recliner, or 'Daddy chair', as she called it, as a first step toward collecting things to put in her future house.

For the next two years they always danced and hung out together at the building's summer barbecues and winter cocktail hours, shared sponges and water hoses on car wash day, and established liberal borrowing terms for things like coffee and sugar, paper plates and ice. In the summer they'd spend long hours by the pool, and Mary would use her little bit of training to give Keith massages to soothe his overworked muscles, when he overdid it in the pool.

He knew precious little about computers, but knew everything about writing. The weekend she helped him install his new computer, he confided he'd bought the thing to finish the novel he'd been working on for five years. She scanned the completed pages--311 of them--and put them in his word processor so he could start where he left off. Meanwhile, he wrote two or three 'how-to' books directed toward adults who were going back to school, things like *The Basics of Studying*, and *How To Attack a Term Paper*, which Mary published. The books sold surprisingly well.

He didn't date much, which was not surprising considering his looks. Women tend to presume a guy that astoundingly hot must have a gazillion other women lined up all the time, so the result is that very few ever get up the nerve to ask. Keith didn't try too hard himself, because it was so easy to rent a movie and knock on Mary's door. Only twice or three times did she notice his potted plant was moved. This was their pre-arranged signal for 'do not disturb.' Every apartment had a potted plant by the door, and hers never moved once. They had a nice, comfortable relationship. They were buds. Friends to the end, they said after too many cocktails at the Christmas party one year, as they supported each other, walking crooked down the hallway. They actually shook hands as they went to their separate apartments, waved and smiled.

"You are a gentleman and a scholar, Mr. Astor, " Mary said.

"You are also, may I say, a gentleman and a scholar, Ms. Stevenson." Keith said.

But that's all.

There was never anybody 'in charge'. They were only friends, doing friends things. He went out and met women; she went nowhere much because she didn't have the time. Most Saturday nights, they'd sit around and bemoan the fact they didn't have dates. They double-dated once with one of Keith's colleagues from the school, who had some sculpture entered in a contest related to a downtown arts festival. Keith thought he'd be perfect for Mary, and the arts festival on Saturday afternoon a good first date. His name was Mark and he was in the computer science department. Keith's date was Sheila from Off-Campus Services at "Wahoo U'" as Mary called Keith's school. Somehow Mark and

Sheila paired off and disappeared, leaving Mary and Keith alone again.

They weren't at loose ends for long. Once Mary admitted she'd never actually seen the Space Needle, or been closer to Puget Sound than you could get driving by in a car, that was all Keith needed to hear. He'd lived there all his life and knew the best places to go. They saw nearly everything Keith could think of and didn't get home until 1a.m.

"Usually the first thing everybody does when they move out here is go around and see the sights," Keith remarked as they were unlocking their respective doors.

"I'm thinking Eliot probably took Lynn to see all that stuff. Or Lynn took Eliot, whatever. He never went anyplace a second time." She shrugged, gave Keith a rueful grin and went inside.

CHAPTER TWO

Everything changed when Clarisse arrived. She was tall, blond and model-slender, and even though she hated dancing and never wanted to go to the building's parties, Keith seemed to love her. When he gave Mary the news they were getting married, she gave Keith the obligatory congratulatory kiss, and she realized it was the only time she had ever kissed him at all. She tried hard not to cry. It all seemed wrong. She so much wanted Keith to be happy, and hoped this cold, too-beautiful woman would give him what he needed.

For the first three months, the potted plant was permanently moved, and Mary stayed away. She'd say a polite hello when they crossed paths, but that was all. Early one Monday morning when she was out of coffee and desperate, she made the mistake of knocking on their door. Clarisse answered, looking half-awake and stoned. Her normally perfect makeup was smeared all over her face, and there was something spilled down the front of her silk kimono. "Whaddaya want, bitch?" Clarisse asked.

Mary mumbled an apology and went to the supermarket.

A few weeks later, she was surprised to see Keith in the parking lot one weekend morning as she came back from the grocery store. He'd been checking his oil, and was closing the hood, and aiming the rolled-up paper towel at the trashcan.

He looked up, and smiled when he saw her. "Hi, stranger. How's it goin'?"

This was different. The last few times she'd seen him with Clarisse, it was like he was pretending not to see her. She had learned not to say anything, and she almost didn't this time. Before she could decide what to do, he'd already come over and was reaching into the open trunk, and with one hand had pulled out most of her groceries in their plastic bags.

"Oh, the usual," she said, picking up the last lonely bag he'd left her. "Working." She didn't know whether to laugh or cry, but she did manage a weak smile. She forced herself to look up at him, nothing more than a glance, really, and closed the trunk. "Hey, you didn't cash your last quarterly check I sent."

Business was a safe subject.

"Uh, guess I didn't get it," he said, nervous as she was.

"Shoulda told me. Oh, well, I'll stop payment on the old one, and send another."

"Sure, why not." Apropos of nothing, he said, "Clarisse seems to have disappeared for a few days. She does that." He tried to sound casual.

Pretty bizarre thing to do, Mary thought, and—*why do I need to know that?* She looked at him, puzzled, but didn't say anything. He was not acting at all like a recently married man should act. He didn't seem happy, or settled at all. Once they were inside going down the hall, she said, "Want a coffee?"

There was a lot they weren't saying as she unlocked the door and went into her apartment. Keith set the bags down on the kitchen counter and started to help her put things away, just as he'd always done. He remembered where everything went. For a moment it was like he'd never left her. *Don't think about that*, Mary said to herself.

She made coffee, hoping desperately for something to say. Keith was sitting at the kitchen table, watching her every move as if she was some kind of a research project he was studying. After a few minutes of this scrutiny, Mary looked over at him and said, "What?"

She moved and he was still staring at the same spot. She sat in the other kitchen chair.

He found her hand without looking or even turning his head. It had been four months and six days since they had last spoken. He sighed, a deep, wretched sigh that was almost a groan, and said, "So how are things going with you and Kevin?"

"Kevin? What things?" She had tried replacing Keith with his brother, but it didn't work. There was a depth of character in Keith that seemed completely lacking in Kevin.

Finally, he looked at her. "Aren't you two, uh—"

"Nothing. Went out with him three times. A concert, a really stupid movie, and I don't remember the other one. He came over here the day after the wedding and the only way I could get him to leave was to agree to go out with him."

Keith seemed relieved, an even odder reaction coming from somebody who hadn't been married six months. He chuckled. "That's not the way he tells it."

She hadn't moved her hand, was letting him hold it because, well, she didn't know quite why. "Well, that's Kevin, isn't it? Didn't we always say his mission in life was to get laid as often as possible?" She grinned at him. "I saw what happened with Donna, I didn't really want to become yet another Kevin Astor statistic. Besides, we had nothing at all in common." She patted his hand with her free one, and stood up to pour coffee. "I don't know a thing about real estate, and I really don't care how much money he makes. He took me to a restaurant once, a really expensive one downtown. It was really a nice place, and he probably dropped a few hundred bucks on me, and he was not pleased that I wasn't impressed…"

She was laughing softly, and started to turn around to say something, but Keith wasn't at the table anymore. He was kissing her, his hands all over her under her clothes. She didn't protest as he picked her up and put her on the counter once her clothes were on the floor. She hardly noticed the coffee, cooled from the tile, spilling all over her naked bottom. She didn't know why she letting him do this any more than she knew why holding his hand felt so—fitting.

"You're not done yet," Keith murmured in her ear, and carried her into the bedroom like she was no weight at all. It didn't feel like the first time—more like the last. It was like he was using his fingers and his mouth to remember every inch of her body. He kept watching her face, her eyes, and was laughing gently, pleased, as she buried her face in the pillow to stifle her final outcry.

It wasn't till later she worried that any minute, Clarisse could well be banging on her door screaming obscenities like she did on Keith's door in the middle of the night six times a week. What in hell was she doing in bed with Keith? He was married, for God's sake.

Keith was holding her, with both hands stroking her back like she'd disappear any minute.

She was glad she couldn't see the wedding ring on his finger.

"So, Mare, tell me the gossip. Been to any of the parties lately?" They had to talk about something…

"No, I went to one, gosh, months ago." Not a fond memory, this one. "By myself. Kev was going to go, but couldn't at the last minute. I think he knew I was going to dump him, and retreated to his old game to save face. So I figured, what the hey, I know all these people, anyway, and I was already dressed." She was quiet a moment.

Keith said, "So how was it?"

"It was fine until after the first ten people asked me where my husband was. I guess everybody thought we were married." She barely got it out; she was concentrating on trying to pretend she wasn't crying. Feeling awkward, she pulled away from Keith and reached for the tissues she kept right by the bed these days. She sat up and took a deep breath. "So, I didn't stay long. I couldn't believe they never noticed Clarisse. How could they miss her?"

Keith was pretending not to see her cry. "We—don't go out together much. I can't stand her friends. Half of them are functional illiterates, I swear. She doesn't go out to the pool or down to the laundry room or anything. It doesn't surprise me nobody would see her." Again it was that tortured sigh. "I didn't tell you why we got married, did I?"

Mary shook her head. She didn't trust herself to talk, or look at him.

"She told me she was pregnant. She also said the only way she'd keep the baby was if I married her. Then it turned out she wasn't pregnant at all, she was making it all up. I tried to get out of it. She threatened to kill herself. Sometimes she gets—hurt when she goes out, I'm not quite sure what she does, but she threatened to go to the police and blame it on me. Stupid me, I stayed. She can really do a number on your head. For a long time, it did seem like she was trying to make it work. But lately…she says she's pregnant again. So now…"

She turned around and looked at him. She needed to be angry with him, but couldn't. "What a mess…" was all she could say.

"I've hurt you, haven't I?"

She could allow herself a smile, a tiny one. "At what point were you holding a gun to my head? No, Keith, I can't blame what just happened entirely on you—only 50%. It's only sex; it's not the end of the world. And damn good sex at that."

She looked down at the tissue she had shredded in her hands, reached for another. She sighed. "What hurt was suddenly just being dropped out of your life like obsolete software. One day we're the best of friends, the next it's, 'don't even talk to me, bitch! I'm getting married!' No explanation, no nothing. I'm supposed to be happy for you as you throw your life down the drain for—." She bit back the words she really wanted to say. "Now I'm not even allowed to say good morning in the hallway anymore."

She reached down to the foot of the bed and grabbed her robe. Putting it on, she continued, "I always expected one day you'd meet somebody and gradually I'd be phased out by somebody younger and prettier—I'm not an idiot, and I was prepared to be happy for you when it happened. There's something strange about Clarisse. She minds if you say hello to somebody while you're taking out the garbage, and she screams obscenities at little old ladies taking too long to get their wheelchairs though the front door. She's never been anything but rude to me. So now, go ahead, be mad at me for saying those things about your wife, but it's all true. Kevin won't even talk about her, he dislikes her so much. And you know how he loves to dish dirt. I don't get it." She shrugged. It was hard for her to say these things to her former best friend, but she couldn't say anything else. "We've always been honest with each other, why should I stop now?"

He sat up and put his hands on her shoulders. "Don't ever stop being honest, Mare. I always loved that about you. I can't be mad at you for that. I know what she's like, I know what she does. But I told her I'd take care of her until the baby's born, and the baby afterward, and god help me, that's what I'm going to do." He put his arms around her and kissed the top of her head. There was real regret in his voice as he said, "I hope you can forgive me for the way I treated you. You deserve so much better than that. I guess it was my way of keeping her away from you."

"It's OK, Keith. Really. It was so out of character anyway…" There was no point in making an issue of it.

There was a catch in his voice as he said, "Find your perfect future guy Mare, the one you bought the Daddy chair for. No more dweebs like Eliot, huh? Don't settle—be picky. You're beautiful, smart, and so much fun. You deserve the absolute best, and don't forget it."

"That sounds an awful lot like goodbye. But we kind of already did that."

"Yeah, I guess it is. Everything's different now, the rules have changed. I didn't want it to be this way, but with Clarisse the way she is—I've got to be more careful than careful. I want my baby, Mare, more than anything." He was quiet for a moment as he touched her breasts, her stomach. "Have those babies you wanted, Mare—and do me a favor."

"Huh?"

"Love that perfect future guy. Take care of him. You're so good at that." He looked at the clock and said, "I better get the hell out of here." He got up and went to the kitchen to get his clothes.

She followed him into the kitchen where he was dressing. He was sitting on a chair tying his shoes, with his shirt on the table. She noticed some red marks on his back up near his shoulders she hadn't seen before. She knew every inch of his back from dozens of summer massages. Random rows of four aligned red dots, like recently healed injuries. Farther down was what was clearly a raggedly healed cut. What they were didn't register then.

He stood up and Mary thought, for no reason at all, he's ten times better than Kevin. He held out his arms, with something close to a smile, and she went over for a last hug. Hugs had always been allowed. So softly she almost didn't hear, he said, "I'm sorry, Mary."

She was crying too much to answer.

Then he was gone, the door closing behind him without a sound. He'd been there for exactly 32 minutes.

She sat down at the computer, which she'd placed by the window to give herself something else to look at once in a while. Until that morning, she had gotten the business of the solitary life down pat. She did her laundry and took out the trash at odd hours to avoid meeting Keith. There was plenty of work to keep her busy; after all it wasn't like they had spent huge chunks of time together. Only three or four hours every evening and all of most weekends. Then, out of the blue, poof! He's gone. Just like this morning. And what was that about anyway? She looked out the window, and watched as a stray dog walked down the driveway. Every few yards there was a spruce tree, and the dog stopped at each one and lifted his leg. Mary started to giggle despite her sadness. Was that it? H'mmm.

Now would be the time to call Dad and see what he thought about the whole thing. Or not. As a psychologist, her dad had no trouble at all discussing sex, clinically or otherwise. As a dad, Bob Stephenson was like any other when it came to his daughter.

She remembered one New Year's Eve party in the big farmhouse outside Ann Arbor when she was about 14. She was standing on the front porch for a minute to escape the marijuana fumes, when one of Dad's friends came out behind her and tried to kiss her. Only, Dad was also outside, on the lawn right beside the porch. That was the night she learned her dad was a magician, because a second later, Dr. Estep was in the bushes, and a second after that, he disappeared, never to be seen at their house again. Maybe it wouldn't be such a good idea to ask him about this morning.

And she knew there was no point in even bringing it up to her mother, who still had a poster that said, "A Woman Needs a Man Like a Fish Needs a Bicycle." Her mother also had a T-shirt that said, "So Many Men, So Little Time." Go figure.

At least she knew now that Keith given her a thought before he chained himself to Clarisse, and that was comforting. "Well, this isn't getting me anywhere," she said aloud to the empty room. She showered and dressed and went to the mall. She wanted to be somewhere there were lots of people.

It wasn't till days later Mary figured out what those odd marks on Keith's back were. It was late at night, and she'd forgotten to eat, as usual, and had worked almost ten hours straight. She took a potpie out of the freezer, and was making holes in the crust with a fork when she realized what the pattern reminded her of. She stood there and stared. "Oh, my God," she said aloud. "That bitch!"

She dropped the fork on the counter as if it had burned her hand. She put on her shoes and found her purse, after dumping the potpie in the trash where she couldn't see it any more. After going outside to the parking lot, she sat in her car for a long time before she could calm down enough to drive.

For the first time ever since leaving Michigan, she felt lonely. Her time was taken up so much with work, that even Eliot's and then Keith's presence had been enough. The last few months there were her online friends to fill in the spaces— dozens of them. Some of these people she had known since the Internet was new, and among them were doctors, lawyers, writers, and even an Indian chief. Tonight, though, what she wished for was an in-person friend to talk to, and there wasn't anybody. She didn't even know her other neighbors, because it seemed people would move in and six months later they were gone again. She couldn't bring herself to go back to any of the social events sponsored by management. Too many reminders of Keith. He was always more outgoing, and ironically knew most of the people in the apartments, and always remembered names. Everybody would ask about him, just to be polite.

She found herself going in to a fast-food place, which at this time of night was crowded with teenagers and twentysomethings in serious dating mode. She felt like somebody's mother out to spy on the kids. By now she was so hungry it didn't matter. She was at the point where, if she didn't get something to eat soon, she was in danger of fainting, maybe a serious car accident. After she got her burger and fries, she found an isolated table and watched the kids.

Across the aisle and down a table, there were three couples; maybe seniors in high school, judging from the varsity jackets the boys were wearing. Football players maybe—all big, hefty dudes. Two of the boys had just come back from the counter with food for everybody. Five of the six unwrapped their burgers and started eating, but one girl looked at her burger, re-wrapped it, and set it back on the tray, leaving the rest of her food untouched. She was pretty, with dark short hair. The kind of pretty that doesn't last, judging from the amount of makeup she wore. She took a lipstick and a mirror out of her purse and began fixing her makeup.

Her date said something Mary couldn't hear, then laughing and shaking his head, picked up the girl's burger and went back to the counter. He brought back another. The girl looked at the burger, waited until the boy sat down, got a sip of his drink, then handed it back. She was watching him in the mirror each time he took the burger back. Two more times the pantomime continued, and the rest of the group was nearly finished eating. The last time, the boy looking frustrated by now, his burger with one bite out of it sitting on the table, sat down.

The girl threw the burger back at the tray, knocking the boy's drink over and spilling it, and shoved him out of her way as she got up, her big shoulder purse sweeping the rest of his food onto the floor. "You don't care anything about me, Jason!" she shrieked, and everybody in the restaurant turned and looked as she stalked out the door. Jason picked up the mess, and followed.

Through the window Mary could see the girl standing outside, out of the line of vision of her friends. Her arms folded, she was swinging her purse by the strap with one hand. She wasn't very tall; close to the size Mary had been herself in high school, when her weight was still in two digits. As Jason approached, by the girl's movement Mary could almost predict what would happen next. The arc of the swinging purse was getting wider and wider, and as Jason got in range, she lifted it, aiming at his head. When the purse made contact Jason staggered, put out a hand to steady himself against the side of a van, and the alarm went off. Both of them moved out of Mary's view. Mary wondered what on earth had been in that purse.

After she had eaten, Mary felt a little better. She left the restaurant, passing the group lingering over their drinks. She could hear one of the girls saying, "She's a fucking bitch, dunno why he puts up with it."

Good question, Mary thought. *Why does he put up with it?*

When Mary got home, she went online and went to her favorite chatroom and started asking questions. To her surprise, her buddies who between them, she once said, knew everything, had no answers for her. Most of them were guys, too. So she went surfing on her own. She first found some websites devoted to things like child custody and divorce.

At 35, she had seen her share of friends divorcing, and she had never understood why things couldn't have been decided more equally. Women aren't necessarily any more equipped to raise children than men are; she knew that from personal experience. It had been her dad that was the nurturer in her family. When she was little, it was always Daddy that she ran to for comfort when she fell down and hurt herself. It was Daddy that made sure she had her lunch money and both her mittens when she went off to school. Her mother didn't 'relate' to her until she was at least 12.

Even fewer among the websites were a handful of pages devoted to men who had been, or were, being abused by their wives. Their stories shocked her, but she was compelled to read the accounts of control, brutality, and midnight attacks. Dante himself could not have conceived any worse. Long after the sky through her window was turning from black to grey, she had to log off because she was crying too hard to see. She kept seeing those four red dots in a row, on Keith's shoulder…

Another few months, and it became obvious, even seeing her neighbors so seldom, that Clarisse was pregnant. Clarisse was not happy about it, either, as Mary tried to congratulate her during an unfortunate encounter in the hall.

"My life is over," Clarisse intoned. "What do you know about it? Thanks a lot for caring." Her voice was full of sarcasm.

Mary had no idea what was meant by that, but she caught a glimpse of Keith's haunted face as she left and ran to her car. "Friends to the end," she mused, as she put the key in the ignition. "Not a thing I can do about it." She briefly considered calling Keith's brother and asking him out, but pumping the guy for info seemed like the wrong thing to do. Kevin would tell all he knew, no doubt, but he was still more interested in Mary than she would've liked. Nope, not the way. She didn't want to risk raising his hopes again, or finding herself ending up like Donna, if she was curious enough to say yes, and sleep with him.

All she could do was stay out of it. She wondered for a brief, insane instant what would happen if she stopped into the college during Keith's free period—nope, not that way, either. They had said their good-byes. This was not her business.

She had learned to work with the radio on at night—then to sleep, she'd use the headphones to block out being startled by Clarisse banging on the door, screaming at Keith when she locked herself out. This happened less and less often now, but the silence was somehow worse.

CHAPTER THREE

K eith stood in the hallway, by the door with the potted plant on the wrong side. His door key was in one hand, the briefcase and a grocery bag in the other. Behind his door, he could hear the sounds of Clarisse's favorite TV channel talking about the fashions for fall. He hesitated a moment, looking across the hall at Mary's door. It was quiet over there, and he could imagine her sitting at the computer with her glasses on, finishing up the last bit of work for the day. Next, she'd check her e-mail, then she'd go stand in the kitchen looking endearingly confused for a few minutes while she decided what to cook for dinner.

Just weeks before he met Clarisse, they decided it was silly for both of them to cook dinner separately, so they took turns cooking and had their dinner together every night. They went grocery shopping together on Saturday, and Sunday was laundry day. On Mary's days to cook, more often than not, dinner would be ready when he got home. Sometimes there would be a one-word note on his door, saying something like, "Tabasco?" or "salt?" this meant she had run out of something she knew he had, and would he please bring it with him. He'd stop in his own apartment long enough to change his clothes, dropping the briefcase on the couch like it was the most normal thing in the world.

Now, the couch would be full of Clarisse, the floor in front of the couch and/or the coffee table littered with the remains of whatever she'd eaten—or tried to eat, that day. If she couldn't eat, then the TV dinner would most likely be splattered on the opposite wall where she had thrown it. If she could, the dishes would be empty, lying on the floor. He'd have to step carefully then, because somewhere in the apartment would be a puddle of vomit where he least expected it, which he was expected to clean up. The days when she was both able to eat and keep it down were rare. It was a difficult pregnancy, and the doctor had told them both Clarisse needed to come to terms with the fact she was going to be a mother, if she expected the situation to improve.

He tried to feel sorry for her. After all, this was his child she was carrying. It was difficult, when he knew she didn't want the baby at all. She referred to the baby as "your fucking monster" and wouldn't do anything for the baby or even for herself. He hoped that pregnancy would have a calming effect, and her violent rages would either slack off a little, or go away. It didn't happen, even though he did his best to help her, to take care of her.

For a few weeks, a long time ago, it did seem that maybe they could work things out. For a few weeks, she was the Clarisse he had met at Kevin's party. She was more beautiful than ever. The few pounds she had gained gave life to her silicone breasts, and added subtle curves to her too-slim body. She was charming, sensual, and didn't complain when he wanted to make love to her in traditional ways. She even faked orgasms to make him think she was enjoying it. She stopped telling him to hurt her, stopped shoving him away when he wouldn't. She stopped jabbing those inch-long acrylic nails into any portion of his body they encountered. He almost began to feel comfortable with her again.

The other shoe dropped one day, when she spent less time than usual getting ready to go out, coming out of the bedroom wearing a simple blouse and slacks and hardly any makeup at all. She came right back in when she found her car wouldn't start. Keith was at home, because it was a Saturday, and Clarisse often went shopping on Saturdays or to lunch with a friend. He had gone with her a few times to lunch and parties with her friends, but they were shallow, mindless people who talked about nothing but clothes, sex, and shopping. Every single one of them—even the men—had hit on him at one time or another. Being groped by some sixty-year-old pervert was not his idea of a good time.

He went out to the parking lot, to see if there was anything he could do. While he was getting in to try and start the car, he noticed a plastic grocery bag containing sanitary napkins on the front seat. "What's this?" he asked Clarisse, standing by the open car door.

Her delft-blue eyes widened, and she said in her little-girl voice, "Oh, Keefie sweets, I didn't think you'd mind if I went and got rid of it now, do you? Everything's been so good lately, do you really want to fuck that up?" She knelt down, put an arm around his neck, and started nibbling his earlobe. Her other hand reached down between his legs, stroking. No response.

"You were just going to do it and not tell me?" he asked, furious. He made a move to get out of the car, but couldn't. She had his ear between her teeth and her hand on his balls. "You know how I feel about it. Have the baby and I'll take care of him. That was our deal, Clarisse, and you know it."

She let go of him, and her eyes weren't so pretty anymore. They turned almost black as if something evil had been activated. Later he'd learn to recognize that look as a signal to be prepared. Her voice went down an octave. "You fucking worthless bastard," she said, using both hands to shove him away from her.

That was her first try. The second try was even worse, and he didn't even want to think about it right now. He was exhausted, and hoped he'd be able to get some sleep tonight. She hadn't let him sleep for two days now. Every time he started to fall asleep, she'd 'nudge' him in the back with a nail file. "I can't sleep, shithead, why should you?" she'd whine. Of course she couldn't sleep. She slept all day.

With a deep sigh of resignation, he put the key in the lock, wondering what he might find. She was masturbating, leaning back against the arm of the couch, moaning. She was naked, facing the door with one foot on the floor, and the other braced against the wall above the couch. Her clothes were thrown on top of an empty TV dinner tray on the floor, with the arm of her blouse dangling in a nearly empty glass of soda. She didn't notice Keith come in. With one hand reached around her pregnant belly, scrubbing at her crotch, she was beating her inner thigh with the point of a pen in the other hand. Her thigh was covered with blue ink. Later, she'd wipe her hands off on the couch and watch TV the rest of the evening, questioning Keith's every move.

Even though the sight disgusted him, he knew it was a good sign. It meant she had eaten, and kept the food down. It could be a peaceful night. Maybe he could take the garbage out without too much explanation. He didn't offer her one of the frozen dinners from the bag. She didn't like to be disturbed when she was 'having fun', as she called it. He'd stopped at a fast-food place and grabbed a hamburger at the drive-thru, eating it as he drove home. It wasn't a good idea for him to cook at home anymore. The frozen dinners were for Clarisse, for tomorrow.

He didn't buy more than they could use in a day. If Clarisse was having a 'sick' day, as many dinners as there were in the freezer could end up on the wall. She'd try to eat one, and if she didn't like it, she'd pitch it, then try another and another until they were all gone.

She refused to cook more than nuking something, even to make a sandwich. Concerned that she wasn't getting enough food, or anything really nutritious, he had first tried bringing home prepared salads. There had been a time when she'd practically lived on the things. "So what am I, a goddamn rabbit, now?" she shrieked, and jammed the open container in his face. He next tried offering nutritional drinks, but she accused him of thinking she was fat. She waited until he was asleep, and then poured the contents of all four cans over him. When he awakened the next morning, covered in a sticky mess, she laughed as if it was the best practical joke she'd ever seen. He tried to take the sheets to the laundry room to wash them, and she accused him of using it as an excuse to see Mary. He saw her eyes turn dark, and he put the sheets in a garbage bag and buried them in the closet.

What she really wanted was for him to stay home with her and cook her meals. That was one battle Keith won, though hard-fought. After a full weekend of suffering screaming, tears, slaps and a particularly bad cut on the back, he finally made her understand that without his job, he couldn't pay the rent and she'd have to live with her parents, whom she claimed to hate. At one point she was worked up enough to confess, "If I go there, I'll wanna fuck Daddy, and I'm sick of him! He's boring! He's got this tiny little dick that isn't half the size of yours!" Then she flounced into the bedroom and slammed the door, leaving an aghast, revolted Keith sitting alone in the living room.

"Keefie sweets, I gotta take a leak—will you get me to the bathroom?" Her little-girl voice, which he had thought cute once, for about five seconds, came from the living room. He closed the freezer and went in to help her up. She lived on the couch, only going to the bedroom for the occasional change of clothes and to try to bully Keith into having sex with her. He wouldn't—never again. In fact, he never even removed his clothes any more, except behind the locked door of the bathroom. It wasn't so much that she wouldn't bathe, or that he was forced to watch her kind of masturbation several times a week. No, it was the item in her bottom drawer that scared the shit out of him.

One night, back when he still cooked at home, she surprised him by offering to set the table. Not long after dinner, he started to doze in his chair. Clarisse urged him to go get in bed. He was beat from a long day, and bed seemed like a brilliant idea. She had as usual when she was up to something, waited until he was asleep, and handcuffed him to the bed. She had put something in his food to make him sleep. By the time he came to, he was being raped with an electric vibrator. It was a cheap plastic thing with a sharp edge cutting in to him. Talking to her—even yelling didn't work any more. It was like she didn't understand words sometimes when she got in her moods. All he could do was groan in pain, which Clarisse mistook for passion. He couldn't walk well enough to go out to the school for two days, and it was a week before he fully recovered. She wouldn't let him change the sheets, which were streaked with blood. They stayed on the bed for a month—a constant warning to be careful, to do what Clarisse wanted.

As he passed the front door on the way over to the couch, he caught a whiff of onions and garlic coming under the door. Across the hall, Mary was cooking dinner. He paused for a second, thinking of Mary in her blue jeans and that pretty white sweater she used to wear. The memory made him feel like he'd been kicked in the chest.

"Keefie!" The voice was low, threatening. "If you don't get your ass over here, I'll hafta piss on the couch!" She would, too.

"Sure, Clarisse," Keith said, his voice exhausted. He went to the couch to pick her up.

CHAPTER FOUR

Another three months. In the morning as Mary opened her door to get the paper, she found a sticky note on the door, in Keith's handwriting. "John Jacob Astor," it said. "4lbs, 11ozs. Early and little." Oddly, it was signed, "Love, Keith."

Love, huh? Friends to the end. They had always left each other notes on their doors. Reminders. "Don't forget the barbecue tonight." Requests. "I made salsa. You got chips?" "What was the name of that William Blake poem?" Answers to previous notes. "Sorry—too short for volleyball! Call ya when I grow!" They were never signed; they knew where they came from. With Clarisse in the hospital, it must be OK to leave a note again.

She took some flowers to the hospital, but Clarisse was sleeping, and her mother was standing guard. Mary had seen her before on the patio at Keith's, shortly after the wedding. The mother was one of those who thought gobs of makeup could erase the years of bad living and nothing to do but party. Her hands reminded Mary of jewels on a skeleton as she took the flowers, asking "You one of the hotshot Astor sisters?" in a raspy voice, like she was telling a door-to-door preacher to go away.

Keith had no sisters. Mary couldn't understand why his mother-in-law wouldn't know that, and it irritated her. Besides, she was far too short to be an Astor. Even the wives were much taller, much prettier. She left the flowers and went home. Daddy was presumably in the Neonatal Unit with the baby, so there was no hope of seeing Keith. Not being a family member, and not seeing any of the more-friendly Astor family about, there was no point in her hanging around.

Mary caught up on sleep, and even gave up the headphones. It was something about Clarisse being away that somehow let her relax. One night she realized that she was completely out of coffee and she'd better get some for morning. There was nothing worse than waking up and having to drive to the store on no coffee at all.

She grabbed her purse and headed out the door. Keith almost fell in from his position huddled in her doorway with the baby, sitting on the floor. Keith had a cut over one eye, and the beer-soaked shirt told her she'd walked into the last moments of what had to have been a nightmare. He struggled to stand up, holding onto the baby for dear life.

"Let me take him," she said casually, when she could see him having trouble standing up with the baby in his arms. For an instant Keith drew away, his hands going around the tiny bundle in a movement of protection. He looked up at her, and she saw the fear in his eyes replaced by something else that looked like relief. This was Mary, his bud. Friends to the end. She could hold his baby.

The little guy squirmed as Mary picked him up, but didn't cry. He looked around in that dazed way newborns have and went back to sleep. He was so tiny Mary could hold him in her own small hands. Mary knew nothing about babies, but this one charmed her. It was the first time in her life she'd ever held a baby, anyway. She was surprised to find she was having a physical reaction to this child.

Keith stood up, weary, and leaned against the doorframe for support. Mary knew right away he hadn't been drinking—all the beer was on the outside. His wide shoulders were bowed by trouble. Mary had always needed to look up to talk to him, but tonight he seemed shorter, diminished somehow. "Looks like he likes you," he remarked, with the pleased familiarity of a father who knows his child. He lifted a hand to ruffle her short hair like he used to, when they were buddies, and his hand stopped at her cheek. For some reason it felt like an apology. Again?

Mary felt a compulsion to hug him, because she hadn't seen him in so long, but with her hands full of baby she didn't know what to do. Instead, she asked, "Come on in--What happened?"

Keith looked exhausted, battered, and too thin standing in the hall. His eyes were a dull black, with dark circles under them. He hadn't shaved in so long he was close to having a beard. He picked up a pile of baby stuff she hadn't seen that was behind him. He came in Mary's apartment, setting the diaper bag and car seat on the kitchen table, bassinette on the floor. "He's going to want his bottle pretty soon," he said, moving to take the baby back like this had been his job forever.

"And what you want is a shower and some sleep," she said, not willing to let go quite yet. The baby was adorable.

"Well, my idea was to ask if you'd give us a ride out to Kirk's, at the lake. Clarisse took off again. But she's got my keys, so I can't drive the car, and now I can't get back into my place either, and I really don't want to wake up the manager."

"Keith, it's after midnight, and it's an hour's drive out to Kirk's, and then you want to get Kirk and Vickie up? I'm wide awake. Why don't you just get a shower and crash here?" In the old days, it wouldn't even have been a question. She'd spent enough nights at his place for one reason or another to owe him one.

It was surprisingly easy to get Keith to stay at her place, stunned and in shock as he was. She suggested he could sleep in her bed for a while, because she knew the couch here was far too short for him.

"If you wouldn't mind, Mare, just watching him for a few minutes? I do really need a shower." The guy was almost asleep on his feet.

"I'll take care of him for awhile." She rummaged in the diaper bag for the single bottle of formula, and headed to the kitchen.

Keith got up to help, and watched as she pulled a pan out of a cupboard, set the bottle and some water in the pan and put them on the stove. One handed, with the baby on the other arm. "Seems like you know what you're doing," he said, surprised.

"I don't—I'm faking it." This was true. She was doing a good job of it, though. "Go get a shower, huh? That cologne you're wearing is overpowering."

He nodded, but didn't move. "Um, Mary, uh—thanks."
She smiled, winked, and started to give him their old punch on the arm when she thought—maybe not. She patted him on the shoulder instead.

He went into Mary's bathroom, and showered for a long time. The hot water felt good, and there was nobody banging on the door, nobody yelling at him to hurry up. He used one of Mary's silly-looking turquoise disposable razors and shaved for the first time in—he didn't remember the last time. *Astor, you look like a fucking bum,* he thought, when he caught a look at himself in the mirror.

Keith was so tired he couldn't think straight. How long had it been since he'd had a full night's sleep? He couldn't remember. He dried off with a fluffy, soft towel and sat on the edge of Mary's bed, listening to the welcome sound of her warm contralto voice, as she talked to the baby like she'd talk to anybody else...

It was the biggest bed he'd ever seen in his life, and it took up nearly the whole room. It was covered with a deep maroon bedspread, heavy, satiny to the touch. She had a mass of ruffled and lace pillows piled at the head of the bed, all crisp white.

He started to lie down, but almost couldn't when he smelled the freshness of the spread and the pillows, like somehow he'd mess it up. But he'd been in this bed before. When? He couldn't figure out why he didn't remember that, either.

He knew, instinctively, that Mary would leave him alone, as he slipped between the soft, cool, sheets. He could be all right here. He was only dimly aware of Mary bringing the bassinette with the baby into the room, and leaving it only a foot away. He thought Johnny would be OK if he closed his eyes for only a minute...

She set up the bassinette in the bedroom near Keith, so he'd see it right away if he woke up disoriented. She knew he wasn't himself, for sure. After she fed and changed the baby, she left the two of them sleeping, and went to the grocery store for more formula, real-sized containers of the powders and lotions, like the hospital-issued samples she had found in the diaper bag, and some actual food for breakfast. Her usual cold poptart and instant coffee wouldn't do it this time. Maybe he'd tell her what happened in the morning. Right now she suspected, but would leave it to Keith to bring it up.

As she returned from the store with her bags of infant supplies and food, she realized she should have been tired, but wasn't. She felt like she'd awakened from a good night's sleep. She cleared off her couch, which had become a repository for unread mail, books, and computer software, and found her extra blanket, just in case. She washed out his beer-soaked clothes in the bathroom and hung them up to dry.

She went online and found out enough about newborn infants to get her through whatever the next while would bring. As she suspected, it wasn't all that hard. Every couple of hours, Johnny would stir, she'd give him what he needed by the light coming in from the parking lot, hold him for a while, put him down again.

In a way, it was kind of fun to sit on the floor by the bed in the near-dark and hold this tiny, wondrous creature. He was better than any puppy or kitten she'd ever held. It may have been more comfortable to sit in her big recliner in the living room, but she didn't want to take him too far from his dad. It wasn't the baby she was concerned about, it was Keith. No, the baby was comfortable. For some reason she felt that this was a little person she knew, a guest in her home. But Keith--well, whatever it was he'd been through, it was enough. Mary didn't want to cause him an instant's worry. She knew he was a sound sleeper, and her soft voice as she told Johnny fairytales would not be enough to penetrate Keith's fog of exhaustion.

By 10 o'clock on Saturday morning, her energy began to dwindle. She leaned her head against the side of the bed and nodded off for just a minute, while sitting on the floor with the sleeping baby in her lap. She felt a hand on her shoulder. "Hey, Bro," he said softly. "Whatcha doin' down there?"

She woke up a little, and said, "Just keepin' an eye on the munchkin." She'd forgotten that's what they used to call each other. Bro. She missed that.

"You never went to bed, did you?"

She shook her head, yawning. "He's a real party animal, we were having too much fun."

"I'll bet," he chuckled, reaching down and scooping up the baby, who was also waking up. "Hey, did you keep Auntie Mary up all night with your wild partying?"

Johnny had nothing to say for himself.

With one hand clasping the baby to his bare chest, Keith nudged Mary with the other. "Get your butt up here and lay down—this thing's big enough for all of us. Christ, it's big enough for a football team—how come this massive king-sized bed? And how come I didn't notice it before? Was it here then?"

Mary shrugged as she made her way over to the other side. She was a little embarrassed about it. The last conversation they'd had in here had been Keith telling her to find somebody else, and now she really didn't know where she stood anymore. Now she was the one that was too tired to think.

"Ooh, don't tell me—you have a football team now?" he was grinning, kidding. He couldn't say what he wanted to say. Not right now. He wanted to hold her, touch her shining brown mahogany hair. But that wasn't their way. Once, they had made love in this bed. Only once. Did that change everything? Or what?

"You know I don't," she managed to say, but she was finding it hard to look at him.

"Yeah, I know," he said, his voice quiet. "The plant never moved once. I looked every morning, even though I hated to. I was so scared you'd find your perfect future guy, even though there wasn't a damn thing I could do about it. I missed you, Mare." He was so wrapped up in the comfort of Mary's big bed he'd forgotten he was stark naked.

When she sat down on the bed, she tried not to react in horror when she saw his back and shoulders were now covered with bruises and cuts in various degrees of healing. She said instead, "I missed you, too. I thought—well, you know what I thought." Did they always talk around things like this? She didn't think so.

He knew what she saw, but he couldn't say anything about it directly, either. How could he ever make Mary understand how insane it had been?

"I'm sorry Mare." He was adjusting the baby's little shirt, not looking at her.

"For what?"

"For being stupid—a lot of things. Stupid to the tenth power." He looked over at her, his eyes asking forgiveness.

She stretched out on her side of the bed, and there was still an acre of space and the other woman's child between them. She had to say something. There had never been any elephants in her living room. "She really hurt you, didn't she?"

Silence. Some things are too damn hard to talk about, even to your best friend. He didn't know how much it would hurt her to know.

Eventually he said, "Shit. She really wanted me to hit her, Bro, is what's so weird. I did—once. We were both pretty damn drunk, it didn't seem wrong for some reason. She has this way of making me do things I don't want to do. It was so fucking horrible, I slapped her hard, and I just hated the way it made me feel. She—she loved it." He shuddered. "That was the night we made him." He put a hand on the baby's tiny head in a gesture of love. "I couldn't do it ever again, but it was like all she wanted. So she started in on me. Guess she was trying to make me pissed off enough to fight back. Shit, I just couldn't."

He lay back, wincing from his hurts, looking at the ceiling, not wanting to see Mary's reaction but needing to tell her something. Even a thousandth of it was almost too much to tell this caring, loving woman. "I was afraid to leave her, because of the baby. She didn't want him, and tried to get rid of him twice, even though she told me she wouldn't if I was going to take care of him after he was born. She went out to a bar one afternoon while I was at school and picked up a guy. When I got home, he was there in my house punching her in the stomach. I could've fucking killed her right then, she was—enjoying it. Christ. And there wasn't a thing I could do but stand there. Lucky for me it scared the asshole—he thought I might have a gun or some shit I guess, so he left before he could do any real damage. She always kept threatening to call the cops and blame all this shit on me if I interrupted her little games. And the way things are now, I'd go to jail—no questions asked."

"What happened yesterday?" Mary noticed the way he was talking. He didn't use that kind of language, not when she knew him. They had both said there were so many other words…

"She left a syringe in the bathroom. I didn't know about that shit before. She used to do a lot of pills before she got pregnant, I found out, but she stopped for a long time. She was too sick most of the time to go out and get anything, damned if I would. She got home from the hospital a long time before he did, had some time on her hands, I guess—anyway, I found the shit in the closet and dumped it all in the toilet. I've been going to the hospital every day and staying with him as long as I could, and I was just too goddamn tired to put up with that crap. She went ballistic—I was used to that, but she went for the baby with a pair of scissors, and I couldn't…I knocked her across the goddamn room, practically, without meaning to."

The baby, fussing, interrupted him. Both of them said at the same time, "He's wet." They looked at each other and smiled in surprise, some of the tension gone.

Mary got up and found the diapers; Keith handed over Johnny, and lay in bed grinning at her while she made the change. "You don't mind doing this, do you?" Intrigued. Pleased.

"Nope," she said. "He's just one tiny little baby. He's so sweet, not colicky or any of that stuff you hear about. Hardly ever cries. I was telling the truth you know—I was having fun."

"I can tell. You're a natural." He sat up again, and looked around. "That was the first decent night's sleep I've had in a long time. You know it smells so nice in here. How come I was never in the bedroom before, well, you know--?"

"You used to stay out of my whole apartment on principle because I'm a slob."

"H'm," he grunted. "Right now I don't ever fuckin' wanna to leave."

"People change," she said smoothly. "Hey, want some breakfast? I'm starving."

"Yeah, that sounds great."

"As long as you put some clothes on." She winked at him. "They're hanging in the bathroom."

He went in the bathroom and showered again, because he could, and put on the clothes Mary washed out the night before.

Mary was almost asleep, stretched out on the bed when he came out of the bathroom. He said, "Bro, why don't you get out of those clothes and get some rest?"

"I was intending to cook breakfast," she said, her words almost a mumble.

"I think I'm capable of doing that myself. You've been up all night."

"Well, just a couple of hours, OK? I've got things I should be doing." She headed for the bathroom, and Keith took the baby and bassinet in the other room. When he had the baby settled again, he went back to close the blinds and the curtains in the bedroom, knowing Mary liked the room dark when she slept.

She was asleep already, wearing pink pajamas with cows or horses on them—he couldn't quite see. She looked so much like the girls he saw going in to the junior high on his way to work in the morning, he had to smile. He closed the door, but his feelings for her at that moment were hardly teacher-ish.

He went in to the kitchen to make some coffee. He knew she'd been to the grocery store during the night, because the bags were still on the floor. That was one of her little habits. She'd put things away, tossing the bags to the floor, and most of the time she remembered to throw the bags away. If she was distracted by something, she'd go do that and forget all about the bags on the floor. They could have been there all day and night. Laughing to himself, he bent to pick up the bags and a receipt fluttered to the floor. He picked it up, and saw the time it was printed was 3:10 am. She'd spent $42.03 on diapers, formula, baby powder—and all of his favorite things for breakfast. The thought of bacon and eggs was irresistible. He'd grabbed a hamburger sometime yesterday afternoon when he brought the baby home, and that was a long time ago.

About ten minutes later, he sat down to the first quiet, uninterrupted meal he'd had in months. If heaven had a taste, then this was it. Even though some of the microwave-cooked bacon had tiny shreds of paper towel clinging, he ignored it. He didn't want to wait for bacon cooked the usual way. After four eggs, four pieces of toast and two cups of coffee, he was satisfied. He even enjoyed cleaning up the kitchen.

Actually, Mary's place was cleaner than he remembered seeing it. The couch always used to be stacked with CDs—e-books going out, and the books she read herself. This morning it was empty, and the pillow and blanket sitting on the arm suggested why. She most likely had expected to sleep out here while he and Johnny took up her bedroom. Sleep—ha!

One of the nurses at the hospital had joked that he shouldn't expect to get any sleep at all for at least three years. All the nurses in the Neonatal Unit had gathered to say goodbye. They had given him hugs and kissed Johnny, some with tears in their eyes. Clarisse—to whom they referred as 'the mother', if they referred to her at all, had never been in here, had in fact, refused to see her baby. Keith went in every day, staying until they threw him out. The nurses felt sorry for him, and did everything they could to help, bringing him coffee and magazines, giving him the benefit of their combined knowledge of baby care. They'd seen plenty of devoted fathers, but some of the younger nurses had never seen a mother who so plainly did not want her child. "Too bad he's married to that wench," one of them said as Keith was on his way out the door. "I'd take them home with me."

"In a heartbeat, honey," one of the others said.

They didn't know Keith heard that.

Something else Keith noticed, as he got comfortable in the Daddy chair. It was so quiet in Mary's apartment he could hear cars in the parking lot outside. The TV had been on continually for most of the past year at his place. Clarisse watched soap operas, anything to do with clothes, and all the nighttime shows directed at teenagers. At first she had spent a lot of time watching home shopping, but had to stop when she maxed out Keith's credit cards and he could no longer pay the bills.

Mary's remote sat on the coffee table, in plain sight. Keith hadn't seen his own remote in a long time, because Clarisse kept it hidden under the cushions of the couch. When she used to go out, Keith left the TV off and tried to get caught up on laundry and getting the place in some semblance of clean. Clarisse didn't care what the place looked like; she considered ordinary household chores beneath her and flat-out refused to do any of them.

It wasn't easy to get the laundry done; sometimes she'd go out only to come back an hour later when he was at the laundry room. He wouldn't know she was sitting in the apartment getting madder and madder the longer she had to wait for him to come back. She wouldn't believe he was only doing laundry. She could see the door to the laundry room from their patio, and would watch for women going in. She had convinced herself Keith was using the laundry as an excuse to meet women. Once Keith had gone over to do laundry and took a book with him to pass the time, and avoid running back and forth.

There were two women already there doing their clothes, people he knew from the parties. Clarisse went over and looked in the window, and saw Keith talking to them over the washing machines. It took almost an hour and a half for him to get back, as Clarisse paced the apartment and fumed. By the time he got in the door she was enraged beyond reason. She picked up the first thing that came to hand—a fork—and jumped him from behind, catching him off balance and knocking him to the floor. He narrowly missed hitting his head on the coffee table as she stabbed him in the back, shrieking that he didn't love her, they were in there laughing at her, talking about her.

Because it was laundry day, he was wearing an old T-shirt, thin as tissue paper. It was no protection as he lay on the floor, stunned, with her knee in his kidneys. When she calmed down, she threw the fork across the room, and sat back, panting. "You bastard, why do you always make me do this?" she said.

He had no answer. He was wondering what the hell was happening. His shoulder was on fire, and he was only now getting his breath back.

"Fucker," she muttered, picking up her purse and moving toward the door. She took his car keys and dropped them into her purse; her movements deliberate so he would know what she was doing. "I'm goin' out to have some fun, and you better not be fuckin' around on me," she said, slamming the door behind her for emphasis. He lay there for several minutes, with laundry—most of it hers—strewn across the living room floor. Groaning, he sat up and stood carefully, and made his way into the bathroom to assess the damage. He did the best he could to apply some antiseptic, but otherwise all he could do was put up with it until it healed. He'd be sore for a few days, but it wasn't bleeding much, and the tines of the fork had barely penetrated the skin. Or so he told himself.

Sitting in the Daddy chair in Mary's apartment, he began to wonder how he let those things happen. He should have stopped her somehow. But how? That was the second time she hit him. The first time had seemed so much like an accident. She had cried for hours after slicing him in the ribs with the steak knife. It was meant to be a joke, she said, she never meant to hurt him. She was laughing hysterically as she did it, so it must have been funny to her at some point. That one had bled a lot. When he said he should go get it stitched up that had made her cry harder. She was so upset she broke a glass and started to slash her wrist. Keith stayed home, and doctored the cut himself.

He didn't want to remember these things. The baby was stirring, so he focused his attention on Johnny, and wondered what he should do next. He knew he had to get back in the apartment and get some clothes, and his car keys, but his mind would not go beyond those basic things. And he didn't want to do even that, yet. Maybe once Mary woke up, she could keep an eye on the baby and he could get a key to the apartment. Later. Not now.

There was one thing he wanted to remember. While he was making a bottle, he had a brief memory of Mary in the kitchen. She was on the counter, her legs wrapped around him. There was more, he knew. They had ended up in the big bed, but he didn't remember anything about the bed itself. He remembered through a fog, bits and pieces of touching Mary's lovely, perfect breasts, thinking no airbrush artist could create better symmetry. Did he remember it? Or was it only a dream? Sure as shit he couldn't ask her.

The memory kept getting confused with something else. Clarisse coming in the door early in the morning. He sat in his chair in the living room with a last cup of coffee before leaving for work. She was bare-breasted under the leather jacket—apparently she'd lost her blouse. Sometimes she liked undressing in the car, throwing her clothes out the window. There was something about Clarisse wanting him to stay home and 'play'. Then a memory of the pot of coffee being poured in his lap. He had been thinking about Mary—how she would never do anything like that. Like what? The coffee or the clothes?

He shook his head, as if to clear his mind of unwanted thoughts, and sat in the chair again to feed the baby. "It's just you and me now, isn't it, John?" he said to the baby, who hadn't a care in the world.

In the bedroom, Mary laid awake. She heard Keith's deep voice, and the sound of the chair unfolding as he and the baby settled in. She wondered how hard it was going to be to say goodbye again. She should have made the drive out to Kirk's last night. It would have been easier to drop them off, wave and drive back home at 2am. She could have gone straight to bed and pretended, at least for a while, that the whole thing was a dream. She wanted to e-mail her dad, to ask him what to do. She already knew what he'd say. One word—detachment. Be there, but avoid emotional involvement. Yeah, right. Last time it had only been thirty-two minutes. That one was easy in comparison. That one was a quick roll in the hay, so long, have a good life.

This time was different. How could she not be emotionally involved after holding that tiny infant all night? Her dad would say it was social conditioning. Women are supposed to be maternal because society says so, not for any other reason. She could argue that point seriously right now, because she was sure what she was feeling was a natural, instinctive reaction. It was at least partly physical. Her breasts felt heavy, and twice their normal size. They kept getting in the way as she gave the baby his bottle during the night, as she bent to change his diaper. There was something else she'd never felt before, an odd kind of tightening in the pit of her stomach, almost a pain.

When she held the baby she felt happier than she had ever felt before. She never expected holding a baby who was not even hers would make her that high. She couldn't wait to hold him again.

She showered and tried to make herself see sense. Once Keith got his keys, they would be off to

Vickie's and that would be the last she would ever see of them. If there was anybody across the hall, it would be Clarisse, the bitch. Who could predict? Keith might even go back to her and try to work things out. He'd done it before. Keith had been clear that day so many months ago. He had an agreement with his wife, and one night sleeping in Mary's bed wouldn't change that.

She even gave herself a jolt of cold water, to wake herself up. After trying on three bras that all hurt because they felt so tight, she gave up and went braless for the first time in ages. By the time she was dressed and out in the living room, one look at Keith and the baby made all her good intentions evaporate. They were both asleep in the big chair, looking like they belonged there. Well, why wouldn't they? Keith had picked it out. She remembered he had been amazed that she would so blithely whip out the charge card and pay what to him was an outrageous sum for a chair. It was real leather, built to withstand a big guy through many evenings and weekends of channel surfing.

She deliberately turned her back on them and went to get coffee. She was looking down at her coffee cup, trying hard to regain her sense of detachment, when Keith came up behind her. His hands found her breasts under the T-shirt, and he was kissing the back of her neck. Déjà vu. She froze.

"No, not again," she said, even though she didn't want to say that.

"It's only sex," he murmured against her hair.

"Not with you, it isn't," she said, making her voice as firm as she could. She pulled away and went to check her e-mail. The high back of the office chair was between her and Keith, and she wanted to disappear behind it.

"What do you mean?"

"I mean, 32 minutes last time, a few hours now, how long before you go back to Clarisse again? You left no room for misunderstanding last time. I can't just be here every time you have a fight with your wife, it's not fair. We've always shared stuff—but I do mind if you think I'm going to be available every time you get horny. I can't play that game." She hated saying these things, but she knew this morning, even though it was almost noon, she had to be tough.

"Mare—"

"Yeah."

"I don't remember. Last time—I don't remember much of it. I don't know what I said." All he could remember was a glimpse of a feeling that it was good, and satisfying. Nothing before, or after.

She whirled around in the chair and stared at him. "You remembered what I said—it was only sex."

His eyes widened in surprise. He didn't remember her saying that. It just popped into his head today.

"You pretty much told me to stay out of your life, which I've done. You said you were going back to Clarisse, and that was it. It was very definitely goodbye. I told myself it was only sex to make myself feel better. But—but you're the only man I've ever cared enough about to miss that much." Damn—she didn't mean to say that. She turned back around and tried to look at the e-mail, but it was all running together.

"I don't remember you saying that. But, yeah, at first I thought I should try to stay with

Clarisse. A baby needs his mother, too, and I hoped after he was born she'd love him. But she doesn't want to be his mother; she doesn't want him at all. She fucking hates him, Bro, and I can't ever go back to her, because it really would not be safe for Johnny. Or me, either, I don't think."

The shrink's daughter was speaking now. "Probably not. You know, it wasn't long after you were here that I figured out what was going on over there at your place. You told me some of it, but not in terms I'd really understand unless I had more to go on. You probably didn't want me to know. Only, some things happened—" She went on to tell him of the night she spent driving around, the incident at the fast-food place, and finally finding what she was looking for on the Internet.

"You were worried about me?" He really didn't want her to know, but the damage had been done.

"Yeah." *More like blind panic, actually*. But she didn't say that. Instead she said, "Hey, it's Saturday, let's make a pizza tonight!" He wasn't getting any more out of her.
For a while it was almost like old times. Back then it was two single people, working for a living, not many cares in the world. She knew he liked his coffee black, and cold pizza was the breakfast of choice on Sunday morning. He knew she didn't like artificial sweeteners and couldn't eat chocolate after 4 p.m., or she couldn't sleep. He'd more often than not forget to put bleach in the whites when they were doing laundry, and took so long folding his clothes Mary couldn't help but tease him about it. There weren't many more things they needed to know, but they knew. All of their opinions and dreams were freely expressed for two years. Any

question could be asked, and neither of them ever felt the other was prying.

Both of them were almost comfortable with each other now, though Mary knew Keith had plenty on his mind. He was jumpy. Once she accidentally let her hand drop on his shoulder as she set a coffee cup on the table, and she thought he was going to leap out of his skin. He kept asking permission to do things, far beyond the usual realm of politeness. This was not 'please pass the salt', it was something else. It was more like he half expected she'd really say no. She couldn't figure it out.

Keith said Clarisse's pattern, if she left on a Friday night, had been to stay away until Monday morning. He desperately needed a change of clothes and his hidden spare keys, at least. Mary went down to the manager's office and got him to let them in.

This was not Keith's apartment where she had spent so many Sunday afternoons watching old movies and teaching Keith to run his software. His collection of old framed family photographs that used to cover the wall above the couch was gone, with a big red wine stain left on the wall. There were greasy footprints— *footprints?* on the wall where the couch stood against it. An overflowing laundry basket full of dirty clothes sat on the coffee table. The computer monitor lay smashed in a corner. The black rubber handles of Keith's kitchen shears they had used to cut up chicken protruded from a plastic bag holding newborn-sized diapers sitting on the desk. There was an odd smell that Mary couldn't identify.

The furniture looked sticky in places, like somebody had spilled gelatin on it a month ago and left it to dry. Keith had used his income tax refund to buy the couch and chairs, and Mary had helped him pick them out. They used to be clean and comfortable when Mary sat on them and talked books with her bud.

They had spent most of their time at his place because Keith was a 'neat' and Mary was a 'messy'. Things had really changed.

It wasn't much better in the kitchen, where it was clear they'd been living on TV dinners and fast food for some time, and nobody had taken out the garbage in a longer time.

Keith followed her in, neither one of them saying anything for a minute. He didn't know what to say, and neither did she.

The bed was ruined. It was soaked, probably from the contents of seven or eight beer cans that lay among the filthy sheets. The dresser was nearly covered by bottles and jars of cosmetics in every imaginable shape and size. There were piles of dirty clothes and empty cups and glasses—half of them used as ashtrays on every available surface.

Mary helped Keith carry his clothes and a few personal things over to her apartment. Keith took his computer over to Mary's to see later if it would still work with her monitor. He didn't say what or why any of it happened, and she didn't ask. It was only her business if he wanted it to be. Still, it wasn't easy. Mary was a woman who never asked rude, prying questions, but this wasn't just anybody here. This was *Keith*, who knew by one look if she had PMS or was just having a bad day. He knew how to cheer her up, too.

She had always looked up to him, in ways that had nothing to do with his height. He had always been self-assured, in control. He seemed comfortable with life—good at his work and happy with it. Her own tendency toward shyness disappeared when she was with Keith, because she always felt like some of his confidence rubbed off somehow. Today there was something new there she couldn't quite identify. While they were at the laundry room, he kept looking out the window, and every time someone else came in, he looked up, startled. Though it would have been much shorter just to go through his apartment back to hers, they went the long way around by the front door.

They were folding laundry in companionable silence, back at her place when Keith said, "Mare?"

"Yeah?"

"What do you think she saw in me?"

She looked up in stunned surprise, her mouth wide open. "I can't believe you don't know."

"No," he shook his head. "I don't."

"You're a hottie, Bro."

"Huh?"

"You know, drop-dead, kick ass gorgeous, huh? And it improves with age. Your brother Kirk, he's 40 and has to practically beat women off with a stick. I think his wife's a cop for a reason. And your dad's what, 78 and still a stunner." She was embarrassing herself. She gulped. "Anyway, she wanted somebody as hot as she was, I guess."

"Me?" He looked at her, puzzled for a moment. There was so much more to Keith than that. Then he said, looking down at the impossible to fold shorts he was holding, and tried to fold them anyway. "You know how much of Clarisse was fake? Almost everything. Fake boobs, butt, hair extensions, fingernails. She said she was saving up for a facelift in a couple of years, when she hit thirty. That's why she hated having Johnny so much, it ruined her beautiful fake body. She didn't care about anything else but how she looked. She thought after she made me marry her, she could just get rid of him, and that would be that. Then she'd have me imprisoned for the rest of my life. But I couldn't let her." It was killing him to tell her this, and this was an easy one.

Mary had put it off long enough. Taking what seemed right then like a huge chance, she got up and walked around the table and put her arms around Keith. Her voice was warm and full of caring. "It's all over now, Bro, and you're OK, Johnny's OK, and after you've had some rest and time to think it'll be time to go on. But until then, I'm here, and I'll take care of you and the baby. I love you." She took a deep breath. "I want to make sure you've got whatever you need." She gave him a quick kiss on the forehead and fled back to her spot on the couch before he could say anything about it.

He wasn't surprised at all. It was like he was glad she said it. He tried to reach out to her but she moved too fast. They were moving into what had been mutually agreed as forbidden territory. They used to say, "Buds is one thing, honeys is another." Keith always said that the day after he'd moved the plant in the days before Clarisse, reminding himself. Three times, maybe. Big woo.

Now there was something else to be said, and he didn't know how. What he said, avoiding the issue, was, "I don't think I can live over there anymore."

She understood. She folded another two of his shirts before she said anything.

"Stay here." She tried to say it in an offhand manner so he wouldn't see how much his answer would mean to her.

It didn't work. He knew her too well to miss what she was really saying.

He said, "If you think it's too much for you, with the baby and everything…" He couldn't believe she still wanted him around, after the way he'd treated her. None of Kevin's old girlfriends ever took him back.

She got up and walked over to the open bedroom door, listening for Johnny. "Remember that Christmas we got so smashed at the party?"

"Friends to the end—yeah, I remember." She could see it was a happy memory for him, too. For a second he was almost her bud again.

"Well, maybe I don't want to be friends like that anymore. Maybe I want to be something else." This was the most forbidden of the things they never said. She looked down at the baby, not at Keith, as if she was making sure the baby hadn't been moved, or something. She was nervous, really scared of saying the wrong thing. Maybe it was too soon for him, maybe it was even goodbye…again.

"What if I do, too?" He asked. Unspoken were the words, "I want you to love me."

She heard what he really said. "Then maybe it's all right."

He came over and took her in his arms, both of them wishing they had done this so much sooner. That's all they needed right then, a hug and a kiss. So simple, so long avoided. Keith felt like he'd gone home.

CHAPTER FIVE

The first days after he made the move back to her were wonderful. Both of them had missed each other's easy companionship, it was truly a reunion of old friends. Now they could both come out and say "I Love You," it seemed to help. They had a little time living in a warm cocoon with just the three of them. Keith got some much-needed sleep and real food, and went back to work that Monday knowing Johnny was safe with Mary.

Evenings were easier and shorter than they had been in months, and in the mornings Mary would get the baby and put him in the big bed between them. They'd spend their waking-up time talking about everything but the real problems. Mary told him every tiny detail of her life during the past year—how the business was doing, new books she'd read. She'd ask his opinions of something the City Council was doing, or something going on in the Middle East, and he wouldn't have any answer. He wasn't aware of anything the City Council was doing, much less anything in a foreign country. He hadn't read a newspaper or seen even TV news in months. Mary now had an elephant in her living room, her bedroom, and kitchen. The only thing she made any definite comment about was his language, and even that was done in a kidding way.

"So, did you join the fucking goddam trucker's union or some shit while I wasn't paying attention?" she said. "Hey, if you want, I can pick you up some clean memory at CompUSA."

"That bad huh?"

"Yes, I would say your verbal communication skills have suffered."

They decided Clarisse might be visiting her mother in Palm Springs. Keith called her dad when Clarisse didn't show up for a week and asked if he knew Clarisse's whereabouts. Keith remembered something she had said about a drug run to Mexico, and Palm Springs wasn't that far away. She would need some extra money if she was going to get her body back the way it had been, pre-Johnny.

Sometimes Keith would get up with the baby in the night, and in the morning, Mary would find them at Keith's apartment across the hall. They'd taken all Keith's things and put them in storage, discarded the ruined couch, chair, and bed, leaving only Clarisse's belongings where they were—in piles on the floor. Keith would be sitting on the floor in the empty living room with the baby in his arms.

The fact of the matter was, that even though he was comfortable in that square acre of bed with Mary somewhere way over on the far side, he couldn't sleep. As he sat in the living room, his back against the clean spot on the wall where the bookcase had been, he wondered if he had forgotten how to sleep in a place that was clean and dry, with no threat of harm. Had Clarisse taken away something that was such a basic part of his humanity? He'd heard about homeless people who had trouble adjusting to being back in a house.

Keith was worried that same kind of thing was happening to him. He'd lived in this horrible place in filth and violence, for almost a year. He'd been ordered around, hit, screamed at, raped…would he ever be able to be normal again? How did he even let this happen to begin with?

Shit, he'd fucked up everything. Fucking. Clarisse's favorite word, among about 10 others, and that was the extent of her vocabulary. How could he have let himself get tangled up with her?

He couldn't get the images of Clarisse out of his head. The first time they met…That glossy hair of spun gold, the body that could stop a truck. She seemed out of place among Kevin's friends, ordinary human beings all. Not many women that tall could seem so delicate, so fragile. She'd given him an ethereal smile, an angel allowing the attention of a mere mortal, and he was lost to her charms long before the night was over. Clarisse the first time they made love. Before he knew nothing he did had any effect on her whatsoever, before he knew what an accomplished actress she was.

It was his fault, pure and simple. Thinking with his dick instead of his head. Shoulda known she was the kind of bitch that would dream up a stupid soap opera plot to make him marry her, and that ridiculous, farcical wedding that was like something off some cheesy TV show. Like getting married *was* the 'happily ever after'. Some women are not meant to have babies, and she was one of them. It wasn't like he had nothing to do with it. He was there, God help him. It was all his own fault.

The baby was starting to wake up, and at the same time Mary came in, wearing that oddly arousing plaid flannel nightgown. She crossed the room, and knelt next to him, putting her arms around him and her head on his shoulder. "Bro, are you sure it's a good idea for you to be over here?"

"I suppose not." It took a second for him to get out of his own thoughts and back into the world.

"Come on, and get into bed. You can get a couple hours' sleep yet before you go to work. I'll take the munchkin, all right? He wants a bottle."

Actually, it wasn't all right. He wanted to sit there and enjoy the feeling of her firm little breasts against his arm. Then he wanted to carefully unbutton that nightgown and remind himself what a real nipple felt like, coming to life under his tongue…nope, not here. *Never in here!* Shit, what was he thinking?

He handed over the baby, kissed Mary goodnight and went to bed. Someday, perhaps Mary's magic could make the ghosts go away.

Another of the problems was his family, who knew nothing of his situation. They suspected something wrong between Keith and Clarisse, but even Kevin, his closest brother, wasn't aware of how bad things had been. Johnny had been home only a day when Clarisse disappeared, and of course they would be all eager to see the new baby, and wondering why nobody had answered the phone at his place for two weeks. Mary was at the computer finishing up the last bit of work for the day when Keith came in looking weary and unsettled again.

"I saw Kevin today," Keith said, putting his briefcase on a kitchen chair and sliding the chair under the table where it wouldn't be visible. This was a habit from the days of Clarisse. "I never told them anything, so I had to tell him the story right then and there. Then—then there's Mom's birthday party next week, I'd forgotten all about that. I can't miss it, it was bad enough I had to miss Christmas."

Mary knew about the birthday party, had in fact been to one with Keith two years before. It was second only to Christmas as the family event of the year. More a family reunion than a birthday party, all the brothers came with their wives, as did aunts and uncles and cousins. Local relatives brought their children. This amounted to over a hundred people at Kirk's big house on the lake. Last year Clarisse would have made quite an appearance.

Keith's voice was low and shaky. "I didn't know you were still dating Kevin. Did you know he was planning on asking you to the party? Were you intending to inform me at some point, or did you just expect me to find out on my own?" He was leaning his hands on the back of the chair, fingernails digging into the fabric.

"Dating Kevin?" Puzzled, turned the chair around and looked up at him. She couldn't tell if he was angry or sad. It was so hard to tell anymore. "Sure I went out with him a few times, that's all. You know that." Was that one of the things he didn't remember?

"Are you sleeping with him?" That was the real question.

Before she could answer, the phone rang and the baby started crying at the same time. Picking up the phone, while going in to the baby, she almost didn't hear him ask, "Is that why you won't sleep with me?"

She could only look at him with hurt in her eyes. "It's for you, it's your mother," she said, handing him the phone.

By the time he was off the phone, she was leaning over the bed changing the baby, fighting tears. Keith came in and stood in the doorway, not quite into the room. He didn't say anything, and

Mary knew he was waiting for an answer. His expression was strange—almost like he didn't know what she was going to do next, and he was holding his breath waiting for her answer. She put the baby back in the bassinette, and sat down on the bed before she spoke. He visibly relaxed as she folded her hands in her lap.

She felt like she had something awful to confess, when there was nothing.

"I've told you all of this before. For a while it seemed like I'd feel better going out with him once in a while. Another hottie from the hottie family. And that's all we did. Have dinner, go to a concert, that sort of thing. Dancing with Kevin is like dancing with a freaking telephone pole, and he doesn't want to, anyway. Pretty damn boring if you ask me. He's not you, not even a pale imitation. He doesn't know a paragraph from a pair o' sox. We couldn't talk about books because I don't think he's ever read any. And as for sleeping with him…" she shook her head, and looked up at Keith with tears streaming down her face.

"He was pretty persistent, but I wouldn't. The last time I saw him I knew it wouldn't be him I was making love to, anyway, and that's just no way to get over somebody. Besides, it wouldn't have been fair to him, and I thought he knew that too. I haven't seen him in months, so I don't know what that other thing's about."

She looked so miserable, even as mad as he was, Keith had to sit down and put his arms around her. "So then why--?" he asked.

"I was giving you time, Bro. I didn't want to push you into anything. Just kind of let everything take its natural course, I guess, whatever that is. Everything happened so fast. I wanted to let you be in charge of this one, because six months or a year from now I didn't want you feeling you'd been ambushed and end up leaving me anyway."

Now she was sobbing for real, and had no choice but let Keith hold her, unaware that it was probably the best thing she could have done.

After a while he said, "What you don't know about Kevin, Mare, is that he's got a mean streak. Sometimes I don't think he knows the trouble he causes, because he's got his head up his ass most of the time. He probably had some weird little plan going to see what I'd do if I thought he had you when I couldn't. Fooled him, didn't we?" he reached around her and pulled a cloth diaper off the dresser. Using it to wipe her eyes, he said, while her eyes were closed, "I don't know what to think—you tell me you love me, and you know I want you, but it just hasn't happened. And sometimes I feel…like I'm not quite as much of a man as I used to be. And maybe you thought so…"

"God, that's not it at all!" She sat up and put her hand on his cheek. "You're not any less because of all that—I just can't even imagine the self-control it took to keep from strangling her with your bare hands. Lots of guys would've done it, too. And she could have killed you, you know, but you stayed around long enough to keep your baby safe. To me, that's incredible."

"I don't know what to say to that." All of the anger gone from his eyes, he touched her hair and almost smiled.

"Don't have to say anything. Maybe we should just stop talking and get naked and hope the baby sleeps awhile."

Keith thought, What? Was this sweet little Mary saying let's get it on? Fucking great, man…

85

He raised an eyebrow, mischief lurking in his eyes. "Wanta get it on with a hottie from the hottie family?"

"Ooh, the king hottie, honey, the king…."

The first thing he looked for was that elusive nipple, hidden for too goddamn long, in his opinion.

CHAPTER SIX

O ne problem down, but there were still more to go.

They were both in the big bed the next morning, without a stitch on, hoping the baby would sleep just a few more minutes. Mary was sitting up cross-legged, deliberately letting Keith look as much as he wanted to. He kept trying to talk to her, looking at her face, but his eyes kept straying to her small, round breasts and the rest of her body. Kevin would never see this, and he was pleased beyond reason that this was so. A woman had finally said "No" to Kevin.

"I can't get enough, because it's all so real and warm," he said, stroking her thigh with one finger. "I would've thought you'd be, oh, a little shy about it. You're so prim and proper about everything else. But, damn, you're good!" His eyes had a shimmer of gold in them when he smiled at her.

That look went straight through her somehow. A tiny shiver went down her spine, and she blushed. "It's um, well—I really like your body." She unfolded her legs and stretched out on her stomach. "There's something about being flat on my back, and surrounded by all that strength that really does it for me. And course, how long has it been? Nothing like three years of virtual celibacy to bring out the repressed lust."

"H'm." He chuckled. "I hope you didn't use it all up."

"Heavens, no, I'm sure there's plenty more where that came from." She reached over without looking and gently squeezed his thigh. "Actually, it sounds strange, but it's almost a safety issue. I'm laying there about as vulnerable as I could possibly be, and you're on top and it feels like the safest, best place in the world. Don't even ask me to explain that."

He cleared his throat. "Not to bring up an unpleasant subject, but you realize we didn't use anything—"

"I know. I thought about that for about a nanosecond at one point last night. After Eliot left, I went to clinic downtown and got tested for everything imaginable, since I didn't know where he'd been. Everything was negative. And there wasn't anybody else since then—just you."

"And I'm OK, they tested me in the hospital. All of us were. Aren't you worried about getting pregnant?"

"That would not be the end of the world, Bro. I'm a big girl, I can handle it."

"Well! Cover up, would ya, we've got something important to talk about." It was like every time something good came around, something crappy came by to crush it.

"And what's that?" she asked, while climbing back under the covers.

He sighed. "It's not good, Bro, I'm losing my job." His voice was low, defeated.

"Cause of you-know-who?"

"Yeah, partly. Mostly. I haven't been doing it right, you know, I put in my time… they haven't forgiven me for losing the term papers, and the final exam grades last semester got all fu- uh, messed up."

"How'd that happen?" Mary asked, mystified. Keith was a good teacher, who enjoyed working at the community college because he felt like he was accomplishing something. He could

have taught at a university, or a bigger college, but
here many of his students were adults who were
seriously motivated to learn, and that was
gratifying. It was never a situation of 'putting in his
time' for Keith, and to think he was not doing well
at work was almost incomprehensible to her.

"Well, the term papers were in my briefcase
that somehow 'accidentally' disappeared. Clarisse
brought home some disgusting stuff, vibrators,
handcuffs—you don't even want to know. I found
them in a dresser drawer one day, and I couldn't
stand knowing they were there, so I threw them out.
So to get back at me, she grabbed the briefcase
when I was in the bathroom and dumped it
somewhere. The exam grades—I hadn't had any
sleep for about three days and I wrote them down
wrong. Either that or she altered them somehow.
Two of the students failed that shouldn't have. It
took forever to straighten that out. And I missed
classes when she'd call me up screaming about
something and wouldn't shut up for an hour. Not
good things." Unforgivable things, in Keith's eyes.

"Have you explained the situation?"

He looked at her, and his eyes said it would
be almost impossible for him to do that. At that
moment, she knew there was something far worse
he wasn't telling her.

"There are lots of other schools." She knew
how good he was.

"Not locally—word gets out, you know.
And I don't think I can afford to relocate, and even
if I could there's all that other, with the divorce and
custody. I can't just leave the state with the baby."
Not to mention legal fees, court costs, and a dozen
other things. Getting sole custody of a child is
difficult for a father, even a financially stable one,

which right now Keith was not. Clarisse's threats hung over them both like a sulphurous cloud. They knew she wanted no part of the baby; but how far would she be willing to go to keep Keith?

"What's this "I" business, huh? You know I make more money than you, always have." Easy for Mary to say.

"I guess I did, but it never really seemed important." Not as easy for Keith to accept.

"That's because it wasn't. We didn't need much money, neither one of us ever spent much anyway. We didn't have a baby then, either. Mi casa es su casa, mi dinero es su dinero. Heck with the details."

"And you're spending a fortune on him already." With a rueful grin, he shrugged, and looked significantly at the corner now crowded with baby stroller, playpen, and etc. In the other corner was a little dresser jammed with tiny clothes.

"Well, you didn't have jack over there. I can't believe that woman wouldn't even let anybody give her a shower, for heaven's sakes!" Keith's sisters-in-law, as well as his mother, had all offered to have a baby shower for Clarisse, but she'd refused them all. Rudely. She had been so insulting none of them had phoned her again.

"Babies need stuff, Bro. And he's going to need more and more the older he gets. I told you I'd take care of you guys, and I'm going to. If you hate it, just tell yourself it's all for Johnny." She was at sea here. She didn't know how to make him understand she didn't give a flaming flamingo about the money, and she did not want to use it to entrap him. She wanted to help her best friend.

She sat up and looked him in the eye. "Now, listen to me. I had this plan I started when I was 25.

I had a little bit, well—a lot of money from Grandma. I was going to start my own business, buy a house, meet Mr. Right, settle down and have babies and all that. So I lived like a pauper for ten years so I could save and invest and have piles of money for when I settled down, so I could afford to be a stay-at-home mom, no matter what kind of money Mr. Right made. After former honey Eliot dumped me, I was more determined than ever. And guess what?"

She lifted her hands in the air, for a moment gesturing around the room. She reminded Keith of a nude statue, maybe Venus de Milo with arms, which made him chuckle. "So, I've got the business, and this huge bed and the Daddy chair," She winked at him. "—but where's the house? Do you see a house? No, you do not. But the money's in the bank for one, right this minute. I'm loaded, Bro! So let the chips fall where they may out at Wahoo U, you decide what you want to do and I'll back you up. If you never want to tell another living soul what happened across the hall, then don't. WE can afford to let you live your life the way you want."

She could see he was hesitant, and worried. "Are you sure about this, Mare?" he asked.

"Yes, I am. I know it's a guy thing; you don't want to do this. Finish your book, take up yoga, and contemplate your navel. Whatever. Put your life back together and get used to being a dad. And if you find at the end of it all it wasn't worth it, well then you can blame me, and--." This was the hardest to say. She had to take a deep breath before she said it. "Then if it's hasta la vista, see ya later, I can live with that. But you're a writer at heart, and what I've seen of your work is damn good. You can do that and not have to answer to anybody."

"I've got to think about this." He had to think about this long and hard.

"Of course you do. But anytime you want, go look in the 'puter and you can see how much I actually have. It just - doesn't - freaking - matter. Not to me, anyway. This is what people who care about each other do, Bro. I know it's hard for a guy to let a woman help him out of a financial hole, but all that cash isn't doing anybody any good sitting in the bank. It's going to be hard enough for you to get through whatever's coming without having to worry about money, too. But think about it! It's there, and the way the business is going, there's probably lots more where that came from. And some of it's yours anyway." She prayed this wasn't the wrong thing to say.

She put her arms around him, and saw the clock over his shoulder. "Hey it's getting late, you better get going. I'd better, too."

The baby was beginning to stir, as Keith headed for the shower, and Mary rummaged in a drawer for underwear.

"Oh, yikes, almost forgot," she said later as he was going out the door. "What about your mom? Is she coming over or something?"

"Good thing you mentioned it, I forgot too. Yeah, she's coming tonight, about 6.30."

"Better clean up, then!" she chuckled, looking around at the cluttered living room.

"No, actually, the place looks fine to me." He looked around. No garbage, no food on the walls. Just some books, baby things lying around. Nothing ugly.

Mary did a double take. "Really? Mr. Neat Freak approves?"

"Mr. Hottie Neat Freak to you," he sniffed, and closed the door.

Keith's last class on Friday ended at 4.30, and he should have been home in plenty of time to greet his mother. He was late, and when Mrs. Astor arrived Keith was nowhere to be seen.

Even Kevin would have been a welcome sight at that moment, but she came alone. Johnny was out cold, unfortunately, leaving Mary to think of small talk. Jean Astor was a petite woman; unlike her sons, who got their height from their dad. From Jean they got coffee-brown eyes and her brilliant smile.

"I wouldn't dream of disturbing him dear. Never, ever wake a sleeping baby. Could I just take a peek?" They went into the bedroom, which was at the moment cleaner than it had ever been, despite the clutter of baby things in the corner. "He is such a sweet little thing, isn't he? Just like Keith at that age. I don't see anything of his mother in him at all—by the way, do you know why they gave him that name? John Jacob Astor went down on the Titanic. No relation to us, of course, but we've always avoided that name."
Mary shrugged. "It's been kind of, um hectic, the last two weeks, I really hadn't thought to ask."

"H'm, I'm sure it would be." Mrs. Astor looked at her with shrewd eyes. "And not something you expected, I'd think." It was no surprise to her that Mary would be the one to pitch in and help out.

Mary shook her head. "I never dreamed anything like this would happen. But Keith and I were friends for a long time before..."

"Yes, I remember meeting you at the birthday party two years ago. Keith's so lucky to have a friend like you to help him out like this. And, Keith—is he alright?" It was clear from her tone she really didn't know how bad things had been for him. She had heard of bad women before, those that ran off with the milkman leaving her children behind. It wouldn't occur to her that women could actually be capable of raising a hand to their husbands.

"I think he will be. He needs some time, but I've been able to get him to talk about it a little, and that's a help."

"Did that woman actually try to kill the baby, or is that one of Kevin's exaggerations?" For Jean Astor, this was something the just didn't happen in the real world. Mothers loved their children; defended them if necessary, but never, ever harmed them.

"No, Ma'am—"

"Jean, please."

"Jean. Kevin wasn't exaggerating, Clarisse didn't want a baby at all, and she blamed him for ruining her figure. All she was wanted was Keith, because, um..."

"Because he is devastatingly handsome, just like his father." Jean said with cold distaste in her voice. She had been down this road before. Her three other married sons had been lucky to find women who could look beyond the physical and love the men they were, inside.

"Yeah, and the rest of them, too!" Mary was blushing. "But somehow, Keith doesn't seem to know it."

Jean saw the blush and understood volumes about Mary. "They're late bloomers, dear, that's why. Even into his twenties, Keith was still too thin and all ears." She chuckled. "And Keith was so serious about school and his writing, he didn't notice—but you can bet the girls did."

"Oh, no doubt. A few days ago I told him Kirk married a cop for a reason—" Mary started to giggle in her nervousness, and Jean needing no explanation herself, was laughing too.

"Now, that's a good one, I'll have to tell Vickie that!"

The two women having something in common, shared a good laugh until Johnny announced he was hungry. "Oh, now look what we did, " Jean said, apologetic.

"It was time anyway. He usually wakes up when Daddy comes in, but I don't know what happened." Mary looked up at the clock, worried. By now it was almost seven.

"Keith used to do that. Didn't matter what time it was, he'd hear Daddy's voice and be instantly awake. Later on, it can be a problem, especially if Daddy's working late, but at least you don't have any other kids. Sometimes Keith would have Kevin awake and it was not easy getting them back to bed! Pete would have to do it, they wouldn't listen to me at all until they'd seen him." When Keith was born, Kevin would have been just over a year old.

Johnny was held and cooed over by his Grandma; happy to see the baby so cared for and loved. "You know, I just loved having babies," she said. "I was one of those fortunate women who didn't have any trouble with it at all. It was like it got easier every time. I would've had ten or twelve but Pete was more logical about it. He was from a family of eight kids, and he always felt he was left out somehow, so five was enough. In fact, we almost lost Keith because he was born so fast! I was standing out on the deck, trying to decide whether the pain in my back was a signal I should tell Pete to take me to the hospital, when suddenly there he was…" She was shaking her head, laughing, remembering. "This little one was a surprise to you, too, wasn't he? So if you ever need any help, if there's anything you need to know, you'll call me, won't you? I don't mean to intrude, but I care very much about my boys—eleven of them now, counting Pete and grandchildren. I'll certainly help if I can."

Mary couldn't know she made the same offer to Clarisse and had been so harshly dealt with Jean hesitated to make the same offer to Mary.

"I'd appreciate that, Jean, I'm getting a lot of information online, but nothing beats having Grandma nearby. My mother's in Key West, and she is not the grandmotherly sort. And you'd know so much better than a bunch of strangers. If you wouldn't mind…"

"Really? You might be sorry, maybe you don't know how grandmas are," Jean warned, with the smile that reminded Mary of Keith in the old days.

"Yeah, I know how grandmas are—they know everything! Mine did, anyway. My parents shipped me off to Grandma every summer almost, until I went to college. So I was pretty much raised by Grandma, and my dad. Mom was busy making the world safe for feminism, I guess, or something. She's only three years older than Phil, you probably don't know that."

"No, I didn't. Was this Grandma your dad's mother?"

Mary shook her head. "No, we never had any contact with Dad's family at all. His parents died young, so I never met them. I'm not sure Mom ever did, either. My mom and dad met each other at U of M—University of Michigan, when mom was a freshman and Dad a graduate student. I'm the child of hippies, Jean, and my dad was a psychologist. Sometimes I wonder if I was some kind of experiment," she chuckled.

In Jean's world, people married because they loved each other and had children to demonstrate that fact. Then they cared for their children, taught them the best they could about life, and sent them out into the world when it was time. Her heart went out to Mary, who it seemed, had never known her mother's love. This girl was nothing like Clarisse, who rejected the entire Astor family out of hand, as if somehow they weren't good enough for her. Clarisse had never even loved her boy, Keith, as she should. Mary, she could see, loved not only her son but was willing to take on the baby as well. The visit was going as she prayed it would.

When she first met Mary at the birthday party two years ago, she knew, and so did her husband, that this was the girl for Keith. They had waited for Keith to come and tell them that he'd asked Mary to be his wife, because this was the way it had worked with all three older boys. When they brought a girl to the birthday party for the first time, this was an informal announcement that this girl was the one.

Pete thought Mary was wonderful, not just because she was so much like Jean herself. Sure, she was small and pretty, but she could talk to Brian about computers and even understood some of Phil's engineering talk. In Pete's opinion, Keith had the best brain out of all of his boys. This girl—well, it didn't matter that she was a bit older. This girl brought out the best in Keith, and Pete suspected he brought out the best in Mary. The night after the birthday party, as the senior Astors lay in bed, they discussed mentioning to Keith that he should marry her quick, because she wouldn't be around long. Some other guy would have the benefit of her beauty and intelligence, if he didn't move fast.

Then Keith had stunned them both with the announcement he would marry that model creature, whom they had never met. It was a shotgun wedding—Keith was only trying to fulfill his responsibility. Jean and Pete didn't meet her until the wedding day, despite their many requests of Keith. When they were finally introduced, it was Clarisse Astor meeting her husband's parents for the first time.

Her parents had rented a convention hall at a big hotel for the occasion—there were over 600 guests, most of them business connections to Clarisse's family. Nobody ever knew what business Clarisse's family was in. Clarisse was pulled away from a minor TV actor to meet Keith's parents. She wasn't happy about that, but was on her best behavior that night.

"So you're the teeny-tiny Mommy?" Clarisse said to Jean. "Oh, how cute."

She turned to Pete. "And you're the Big Daddy Astor, huh? Still gettin' it up, I bet. Shit, yeah, you hafta kiss this bride!"

Jean's eyes were filled with tears as she watched Clarisse kiss her husband, in a way no daughter-in-law would think of kissing her husband's father. Keith wouldn't look at her, though she tried to catch his eye. Then Clarisse slapped her on the butt too hard, hurting her as they moved away. "Way to go, Jean!" she said.

Jean had never cried so much over one of the boys. She had cried when Vickie and Kirk announced they couldn't have children, she had cried when Phil and Brian told them they were moving to Phoenix, and she had cried when Kevin told them he wouldn't go to college.

When Keith married Clarisse, she went home and cried for a solid week. It wasn't right. Clarisse had none of the visible signs of pregnancy, and Jean was certain she was entrapping her boy only because he was a pretty face. Keith would never know what the family went through after the wedding. Kevin and Pete, and Vickie and Kirk were almost ready to call in a shrink because no matter what anybody did, she went through her daily activities sniffling. At night she cried herself to sleep. All of them at one time or another had sat with her on the couch and held her, not knowing what else to do as she cried and cried, inconsolable. Even Bobbie, Phil's wife and the eldest, with her good humor and down-to-earth outlook, was no help. She would talk to Jean on the phone from Arizona for hours and they would both end up crying.

The men thought they were being silly women, jealous of Clarisse's beauty. Sure, she wasn't very smart, but Keith could teach her how to behave herself in public. She was having his baby, wasn't she? He's a big tough guy. Pregnancy is a great leveler—women always get together on that.

Of course it didn't happen. But now there was Mary, and Clarisse was gone. Jean hoped Clarisse would never surface in her son's life again.

Jean was getting ready to leave when Keith walked in, his face ashen, his hand covered by a huge bandage.

"My god, Bro, what happened?" Mary ran to see.

"Keith, are you all right?" Jean asked, as frightened as Mary.

"It'll be OK, Mom." He pulled out a kitchen chair and sat down. "She had a knife. She caught me in the parking lot at Kevin's just as I was leaving. She went home and saw all my stuff was gone. That set her off. Don't know where she's been in the meantime. Thank God she didn't know where Johnny was." His eyes were back to that old haunted look as he put an arm around Mary's waist.

"I think I'd better go." Jean said, upset by something she didn't understand. "Call me, dear, won't you?" she said to Mary, who nodded.

Back to square one. Almost. Only this time, Keith could come home to a spot of sanity and a better idea of what the future might hold for him and his son.

"God that was awful, Mare. She looked like—I don't know, a death's head or something. Looked like she put on makeup a couple of days ago, and it just ran and smeared all over. Her clothes were filthy, like she'd been sleeping in the street, she smelled. I can't believe I ever thought she was pretty. Ever. Oh—" He groaned, resting his head against her breast.

"What's for dinner, I'm starving. Haven't eaten all day."

She kissed the top of his head. "Dinner's nothing special, I just threw some chili together. I spent most of the day cleaning house."

"You cleaned anyway, huh?" He gave her a knowing smile, and looked around. "Looks good. Get along with Mom OK?"

"Oh, yeah, just fine." Johnny was crying to be picked up. "Somebody hears Daddy! Hang on, I'll get him, you sit. We figured something out today—check this out."

She handed Keith the baby, who instantly stopped crying. "See? You used to do this, your mother said. He hears your voice, and he wants Daddy. Doesn't want mom at all—oh! Did you hear what I just said?" she clapped a hand over her mouth.

Keith smiled, though his eyes were tired. "Sounds right to me. As far as I'm concerned, you are his mother. I hope he never needs to know about that bitch."

Mary knew better—Johnny would someday have to be told, but that was years away. She dropped a kiss on Keith's forehead and put dinner on the table.

After dinner, Keith was sitting in the big recliner holding the baby when he said, "You know my mom liked you before, anyway."

"Yeah? That's nice." She turned around to face him in the computer chair.

"When I told her I was marrying Clarisse, the first thing she said was, 'what happened to that little Mary?' Guess she knew something we didn't, huh?"

Mary shrugged. "Then, yeah. But right before the wedding-geez!" she was ready to tell him something, but he already knew.

"You, too? First time you ever kissed me and I didn't want to let you go." He put the baby up on his shoulder, and buried his face in Johnny's little body. "I wanted to grab you and run, but I couldn't." His breathing was ragged, and he suddenly put the baby in his lap, and bent over and cried as only a strong man can do, struggling with emotions that had been buried for months. The baby was confused by this strange happening and began to wail himself. All Mary could do was go over and put her arms around the two of them, father and son, and let them know without words how much she loved them. When he could catch his breath, he said, "God, Mare, what did I do?"

At the sound of his father's voice, Johnny settled down to the small baby language that only parents understand. Mary knew he was fine, and ignored him.

"Not a damn thing, Bro, you did the best you could. It wasn't your fault the woman's a psychotic criminal. She trapped you the only way she knew how, and when her plan didn't work, she couldn't stand it. She can't do anything, doesn't know anything, and apparently nobody has ever made her learn anything. She doesn't care who she hurts or how much, she only thinks she deserves to be worshiped or some sick crap. Maybe her parents abused her, who knows, but there is absolutely nothing you have done to deserve any of it."

"Just seems like every time the last cut heals, she gives me some more. Mare, I am so tired of all this, you don't know—" He was leaning on his elbows, looking at the floor.

"I do know some of it. That sound system in the bedroom is not for mood music for that football team you were talking about. I got it so I could sleep, without having to listen to her coming and going at all hours. I was so worried about you I almost asked Kevin out again to see what he knew!"

"Shit, that would've been the last thing I needed…" He looked at her in horror.

"Well, I know that now, but I didn't then. Saw you and her in the lobby that day, and I thought maybe she was holding a gun on you or something, it looked that bad." She didn't know how close to the truth she was, saying that. She reached down and picked up the baby, now sleeping. "Let me put him down." She took the baby and went into the other room to put him in his bed.

Mary didn't know if anything she was doing was right. She wanted, first above everything, to help Keith get back whatever it was Clarisse had taken. He was not the same man she had spent so many weekends and evenings with, the guy who let her shower at his place when the plumbing was broken. Who promised he wouldn't look that humid August night they went skinny dipping in the pool when the A/C was down. The guy who read one of her e-books, printed it out and gave it back to her with all the mistakes marked in red and a grade of C I. The next day, she drove out to the college and bought one of the textbooks he used in his classes, and spent hours going over it with a red pencil. She then handed that back to him with a big C- on the cover in red. It was a challenge. Two weeks later she published the first of his how-to books. They'd laughed themselves silly over that one. She and her best friend, her bud, her bro.

He didn't know how often she had sat alone in her apartment, wanting to move away, deciding even—tomorrow for sure—and never quite managing to do it. When tomorrow came, she would tell herself Keith and Clarisse would have to move after the baby was born, anyway.

"Bro, you okay in there?" Keith's voice brought her back to reality.

"Yeah, sure, I'm fine."

She went back into the living room, not knowing what to do, and said, "Hey, you're in the big chair!"

Startled, Keith asked, "Want me to move?" He had been kind of watching TV, the remote in his hand.

She realized she was standing over him, maybe not a good idea. Plopping down to the floor, she said, "Um, no, uh, can I sit in your lap?"

Mary asking permission was a new thing. Well, not recent, anyway. He put his elbow on the arm of the chair, and rested his chin on a finger. Looking down at her from this small height, said, "Hey Bro, you're actin' weird. What's this lap stuff?"

"One of my little fantasies. Like the big bed, you know." She shrugged. "Sit in the daddy chair with Daddy." She looked down at the floor.

"So that's it. Come here, Bro." He was chuckling as she got into his lap. Weak little chuckles, but they were there just the same.

"The times I sat in this chair and thought of you…" she said.

"Yeah, I said, buy the goddamn thing and let's go home!" Stronger chuckles now. "Damn, we acted like married people so much, I didn't realize it." He sobered. "But it wasn't me then was it?" He found a warm soft spot to rest his face.

"Nope, that fictitious dude from off in the future, most of the time. It was like you were there to guide me through it, or something. Very stupid. But then I didn't know about the late-bloomer hotties. Should've talked to your mom three years ago."

"Huh?"

"She told me—you guys don't get really gorgeous 'til you're in your thirties—before that, she said, you were 'too thin and all ears'. So you particularly had no idea what was going on, getting degrees and what not. And you just turned 30. I always thought, being kind of a, uh, 7 or 8 myself, you were waiting for a ten to go with you. 'cos you're a 12."

Keith was silent for a moment, then he was laughing so hard Mary was afraid he'd wake the baby, even in the other room. "You don't know Kevin saw you first, do you?" he said, gasping for breath.

"Uh, guess not."

"Yeah it was that pool party, right after I moved in. I brought Kevin 'cos he wanted to surf for babes. You were wearing that brown bathing suit, the one you wear when you feel fat, with that cover-up thing you can see right through. He took one look at you and said, 'now that's a ten!' Right after, his beeper went off, so he had to go back to work. Never got to meet you that day. But I did. Oh, geez…Mary, I love you."

CHAPTER SEVEN

It was nice times alright, good fun for Mary and Keith for a little while. Even their now-hesitant, careful sex was satisfying, though Mary admitted to being a little put off by the baby in the same room. "He's only a month old, Bro. What's wrong with him hearing us loving each other? He's heard so many bad things," is what Keith said.

Bad things Mary could only guess at.

Keith finally admitted that he'd been on administrative leave for almost two months, and he'd been going out every day to put off telling Mary the real situation. He spent his time walking the beach, thinking. Some days he'd have lunch with Kirk or Kevin.

One afternoon he had a meeting with the powers that be out at WahooU. By mutual consent (or at least that's what the paperwork said) his contract would not be renewed. He had five years behind him at the school, so they couldn't fire him outright, but the lack of explanation for the lost term papers, the altered grades, the missed classes gave the college no choice. Even though he was the victim, there was an undercurrent of suspicion toward Keith that made him uncomfortable, confused, and angry. He wouldn't—couldn't explain why things had happened. His circle of friends was insulted and hurt by what seemed to them a sudden, drastic change of character.

Keith had always been willing to go for coffee after work, the occasional basketball game on the weekend, or to dinner at a colleague's home. Now he froze everybody out. He wouldn't accept any invitations to bring his new wife over for a barbecue or attend even school functions that were social in nature. He had taken an active part in school fundraisers, and been part of the speaker's bureau to promote the school in the community. Shortly after his marriage, he withdrew from everything and everybody. Even his friend Mark was rebuffed when he tried to talk to Keith to get some answers to the question of Keith Astor's new, withdrawn character. Rumors were circulating accusing him of everything from abusing his wife to alcoholism, but he would say nothing in his own defense.

Mary found she didn't mind staying home and taking care of the baby while Keith was off walking the beach. The way she looked at it, he probably hadn't had five minutes to himself in the last year. Even the times Clarisse was gone, he was still under some sort of remote control. She had seen that the day she saw him in the parking lot and they somehow ended up in her bed. If long walks helped anything, so be it.

He didn't tell her what he'd decided about taking time off to write, letting Mary cover the finances. In fact, he wouldn't talk much about anything at all. Mary tried to be patient, but she was worried.

She didn't have too much time to worry, because the day of "The Big Party" was looming. Mary had called Jean as promised, reporting on Keith and baby John, and she'd sworn to be there with Keith. One did not say 'no' to Jean Astor. It wasn't like they were one of those dynasties with bazillions of dollars. But Jean was 'The Mom', and having the Jean Astor seal of approval at that moment meant everything to Mary.

Keith and Mary were bouncing off each other in the little bathroom, getting ready for the party, when Mary heard a sharp intake of breath from Keith.

"What's up, Bro?" She looked at him in the mirror, thinking how really cool he looked in that grey suit. She was wearing a simple lavender sheath dress, and four-inch heels that accentuated her slim figure and gave her an air of sophistication she didn't have in her usual shorts and T-shirt.

He had a look of amazement on his face. "Beauty, elegance, loveliness, charm—damn, where's my thesaurus! You are astounding, Bro, and you wonder why I love you? Don't know what you did, but you just cranked it up to outrageous levels. Sure we can't just stay home, and uh…"

She lifted a disdainful eyebrow. "Nope, my dear, today Little Mary's walkin' in to the hottie family! Inspection, dontcha know." She winked at him. "You could waltz in wearing an old T-shirt and a pair of jeans, but this time I need to be better than best."

"And all it took was maybe five minutes and those few little things." He pointed to her modest makeup bag, which was only a tenth of the compounds Clarisse used.

"Well, I have one of those faces where you have to be careful—too much and I look cheap. What can I say?" she chuckled.

He put his arms around her. She noticed he was careful not to touch her hair. "May I touch those secret places which thou dost divulge only to me?"

"That sounds like a quote, or did you make it up?"

"I dunno, just popped into my head."

He was running his hands up under her skirt, and she said, "Nope not now—gotta go!"

"Rats."

"Too bad, honey!"

They were a little late anyway, and had to park at the top of the hill and walk down. Kirk was an architect, and the house was impressive, built into the side of the hill with three big decks on different levels and picture windows everywhere with a view of the lake. There were people everywhere, and they found Jean and Pete standing outside, talking to some friends.

Jean saw them first. "Hello, Mary dear! You look lovely tonight!" she reached out and gave Mary a hug. "How are you, sweetie?" she asked Keith, who gave his mom a kiss on the cheek.

"I'm OK, Mom."

"Pete, Keith and Mary are here," she reached behind her and patted her husband on the shoulder. Pete Astor turned around and smiled at the two of them. Shaking Keith's hand, he said, "You made it!" Turning to Mary, "So you're the little girl who's been taking care of my boy. How's that baby?"

John was asleep in his carrier, and Keith's dad took a look. "Yep, he's a baby alright." He winked at Mary. "They all look like Winston Churchill to me." He put his arm around her shoulder and kissed her on the cheek. "You're doing a fine job, Mary. Keith looks better than I've seen in months. I thank you for that."

Mary didn't know what to say.

Jean smiled at Mary, her eyes sad, and said, "He's right you know. I didn't realize." She must have talked to Vickie. But now was not the time.

"Why don't the two of you go up to the kitchen? Brian and Phil are here already."

It seemed like they said hello to half the population of the state on the way up to the kitchen, where all four of Keith's brothers were standing by the sink. "Little Mary and the Hottie Family," Keith whispered in her ear. "Sounds like an old 60s rock group," he chuckled.

"Shut up, Bro."

Then four pairs of eyes were on Mary. Keith, at six feet two, was the shortest of the five, and Mary felt surrounded by giants. It was like Jean had said, they were all devastatingly handsome. Yikes! "Suddenly I feel very short," she remarked, trying to cover her nervousness with a joke. She'd met them all before, at the previous party, but Brian and Phil lived in Arizona and didn't know her as well as Kevin and Kirk.

"I remember you now," Brian said. "Seems to me you were dancing with Keith a lot the last time."

She nodded. "Yep, that was me!"

"Hail, Mary!" Kevin said, jumping unsteadily down from the counter where he was sitting. "She used to be my girl," he made a point of saying, trying to imply something that wasn't. "You're lookin' good—get a haircut or something?"

"She always was a hottie," Kirk said. "Where've you been?" Kirk had seen Mary lots of times before at Keith's.

Kirk's use of that word almost made Mary lose it. She avoided looking at Keith, who was for sure also trying not to laugh.

"Thanks, Kirk," she said as casually as she could, ignoring Kevin. "I think I'm going to set this guy down somewhere. He's getting heavy."

Over her head, Phil only looked at Keith, grinned and nodded. Approval from the big brother.

Mary went to sit at the kitchen table with Bobbie and Brenda, and Vickie the cop. None of them were beautiful in any kind of standard way, but each had her own lovely traits. They were strong women who were secure in the fact they were deeply loved by their husbands. The Astors had often married women who were large in size, and equally large in character.

Bobbie's short dark hair and ivory skin did not betray the fact she was 50. Her simple, but elegant way of dressing, made Mary realize why Keith and his brothers had sometimes referred to her as "The Empress."

Brenda was a classic Irish girl, with flaming red hair and peaches-and-cream complexion. Not as outgoing as the other two, she was almost fragile-looking, though she was strong enough to manage three growing boys.

Saying shy hellos, Mary set the baby carrier at the end of the table.

"Ooh, the baby!" said Bobbie, Phil's wife and the oldest. "Can I hold him?"

"Sure you can," Mary said, picking up Johnny, who was beginning to come to and look around. "Want to go see Auntie Bobbie?"

They would find that Johnny was one of those babies who liked just about everybody, as his three aunts took turns playing 'pass the baby', Bobbie and Brenda joking about how long it had been for them since theirs were little, wondering if they forgot how to hold an infant. "He must feel very secure," Vickie remarked, nodding at Mary. "He's got no complaints at all. Hey, mom told me the joke—good one!

"You liked that, huh?"

"What joke was that?" Brenda asked.

"I'll tell you later, when those guys aren't around."

Across the room, Keith looked over and met Mary's eyes, and smiled. There was a little sadness in his eyes, and she wondered what that was about.

The women were chatting about diapers and late night feedings, when Keith came over to tell Mary he was going to look at Kirk's new boat. "Want to look, Bro?" he asked.

"No, I'm happy here. That was long walk down the hill, I'm going to take a break for awhile."

"I'll leave the diaper bag right here," he said, setting it on the floor next to Mary's chair. He gave her a proprietary kiss on the neck, which did not go unnoticed by the family, and went with his brothers downstairs.

Bobbie got up and went over to the counter. "Would you like a drink, Mary?"

"Just Coke, or something, that would be good."

"Oh, so, are you breastfeeding?" Bobbie asked.

The three women at the table looked at each other in astonishment. "Bobbie!" Brenda said, "Where's your head?"

Vickie was shaking her head.

"Oh!" Bobbie exclaimed. "I'm sorry, what was I thinking of..." her voice trailed away in confusion. "I didn't mean..."

"That's OK, lots of people think Johnny's mine. I'm getting used to it." Mary shrugged. "Keith even says he looks like me!" Bobbie brought over the Coke, and suddenly she and Brenda decided to have a look at the boat themselves.

"I think I'll sit here and keep Mary company," Vickie said. "I'm sure she doesn't want to go carrying the baby all over."

After the women left, Vickie said kindly, "If anybody's going to say something dumb, it'll be Bobbie. Don't pay any attention to her."

"Really, that's OK. I get stuff like that all the time."

"So, tell me, how's Keith doing?"

"Oh, he's coping, I think. I'm just making sure he gets regular meals, his sleep, and mostly being around. Not much else I can do."

"Some kind of consistency is a big help in itself. Does he talk to you?"

Mary nodded. "A little. He won't talk to anybody else though. We were such good friends before, we talked about everything, so it's not too hard for him, I guess. He's going to lose his job, and he does not want to tell them what went on, why he messed up so badly this year. It had to be horrible, Vickie, when he first came over he was just covered with cuts and bruises. Can't even imagine what she did to him. I don't push, I figure when he's ready to talk, he will."

"You love him very much, don't you?" Vickie asked softly.

"Yes, I do." Mary was sniffling, and rummaging in the diaper bag for a tissue.

"I don't mean to upset you."

"That's alright, I wanted to talk to you." Mary wiped her eyes before she said, "Clarisse has some strange friends. She used to go out, and be gone for days, and she'd come back home, all bruised and beat up. She threatened to blame it all on Keith, when he tried to leave her. That's why he stayed in the first place, he was afraid he'd end up in jail for nothing. And I'm so afraid that could still happen."

Vickie sighed. "Yes, unfortunately, that could happen. She could also try to get custody of the baby, too, though why she would—I don't know."

"Yeah, Keith went to talk to a lawyer about filing for divorce and he hasn't told me what the lawyer said. She never wanted the baby at all, but what if she uses him to get to Keith? I just don't know." She shook her head, and deciding to confide something, looked up at Vickie. "You probably don't know this, but I've got lots of money, I could very easily just pack us up and go. Just about anywhere. It is so tempting, even now. He's not safe anymore. She doesn't know he's living with me yet, but she could find out. Even if we moved she might find us."

She put the baby in his carrier, and took a sip of her drink. "I don't know what I'd do if she showed up at my place and tried to hurt either one of them. I—"

Vickie put her hand over Mary's on the table. "You don't want to tell me any more about that. I may be his sister-in-law, but I'm still a cop. Don't think you'd have a level playing field because you're another woman, either. Keith doesn't know I've kept an eye on this from the beginning, but I have. I've known for a long time something wasn't right." She leaned back in her chair. Deliberately changing the subject onto less difficult things, she said, "Now, anyway--why does he call you Bro?"

"We've always called each other that. That's more like what we used to be, we said we were friends to the end. Bros. We never slept together or anything, we just hung out together." She chuckled.

"Even though Kirk came over that time to get his book back, and we were sitting there having breakfast, I'd spent the night on the couch because they were working on the plumbing at my place. We never, uh, got together, until lately."

"Now that's hard to believe!" Vickie laughed.

"Hey, we hardly believe it ourselves! It's kind of complicated, but it has to do with partly, the fact I'm five years older—"

"Really? I had no idea!"

"Oh, thanks, and um—"

"Let me guess, I know what's coming here—the same thing they all have, right?"

"Yep."

"And you didn't feel like you were pretty enough for him, yadayadayada." Vickie nodded, pointed to herself. "Me, too. Been there, done that. So did Bobbie, Brenda and probably even Jean. But you know what? With the exception of Kevin they all are fairly bored with the whole idea."

"Jean said it was because they're late bloomers."

"Oh, you've had that talk, have you?" Vickie grinned, delighted. "Good for you, sweetie. That means Jean knows you're serious about him. Because even though it all seems sudden, it isn't, is it? All he did was go back to the woman he really cared about in the first place. Good thing you were there when he needed you."

"I'll second that," Keith said, hearing the last bit of the conversation as he came in. He put his hands on Mary's shoulders and kissed the top of her head.

Vickie got up and went to make another drink. "Something else you need to know, too.

These guys—Kirk's this way, and I know Brian and Phil are, tend to devote all their attention to the woman at home, sometimes to the exclusion of everybody else. You get really self-contained, the two of you in your own little comfy world, to the point where you look around one day and you don't have many other friends. It's not like they make us stay home, not at all. It's more like; you'd rather spend your time with him than anybody else. Sure I see people at work all the time, but the only real friends I have are Bobbie and Brenda. God, you should see my phone bill! But it's also nice to know he's not likely to look at another woman, once he's settled." She grinned. "Anyway, if you find yourself wanting to talk to a girl, either call me or come and find me—you know where the shop is. OK?"

The Astors were doing their best to make Mary feel wanted, and Mary was relieved. "Sure Vickie, I will."

"Now, if the seminar is over, ladies, " Keith grinned, "Mom's about to cut the cake. She's waiting for you. Have we got that thing?" He was looking in the diaper bag.

"What thing is that?"

"The thing you hang the kid in."

Mary found it, and helped Keith get strapped up and put the baby in.

"Want to go for a ride, John?"

As they all went downstairs where the rest of the family was assembled, Vickie remarked. "I've never figured out why she does this—cuts the cake first, and then we eat."

"I think that's from when Phil and Brian were little—that way they'd have their cake and leave the adults alone." Keith chuckled.

"Well, that makes sense, none of the kids really eat, anyway." Vickie said.

The cake cutting and dinner took place on the bottom deck, also the biggest, where there was plenty of room for everybody. Tables were set up out in the yard, which was decorated with strings of lights. Later, the buffet would be cleared away, leaving room for dancing.

A few of the more distant relatives, who hadn't heard the news, called Mary Clarisse, but she took it in good nature. One of Keith's elderly aunts sniffed, "Never did like that blond woman anyway, all she did was sit in the corner, and never talked to anybody." Apparently Clarisse hadn't made such a splash as Mary thought. After dinner, there was more 'pass the baby', where nearly every female member of the Astor clan wanted to hold Johnny. At times Mary wasn't sure where he was.

"Relax, Bro, don't be such a nervous mom, it's all family," Keith told her, when she started looking a little concerned. "They'll bring him back the minute he's wet."

"He's right," said Brian, seated on Mary's left. Brian was Brenda's husband. They had left their three school-aged boys at home in Arizona. Brian and Mary had been talking about computers, while Keith, paying attention to every word, tried to understand what they were saying. "Happens every time there's a new baby, and there hasn't been one in a while, so he's a big hit, I'm sure. Anyway, so there I am with a passed-out tech and a dead computer—"

Mary left Brian to explain himself to Keith while she went upstairs to get the baby carrier, so Brenda could keep an eye on Johnny while Keith and Mary danced. The kitchen, on the top floor, was quiet, except for Kevin sitting at the table, with a bottle of bourbon and a glass. Mary didn't have much to say to him, and when she reached for the carrier, sitting on the table in front of Kevin, he grabbed her wrist. "Shoulda stayed with me, and found out what a real man is like," he said.

She tried to pull away, and couldn't. "Don't—Kevin, you're hurting me."

"How come you want to live with a weenie asshole that lets a woman beat him up, huh?'

Still struggling, Mary said, angry, "Keith's twice the man you are—."

She would've said more, but Phil walked in and said in a threatening voice, "Leave her alone, Kev. You're drunk. Either go downstairs and sleep it off or go home."

Without a word, Kevin gave Mary a vicious look, pushed her arm away and left the room.

Phil said, "The little shit, I don't know why he has to be that way. I'm sorry about that. Are you all right?"

"Yeah," she sniffled.

Phil handed her a paper towel off the roll on the counter. "Hey, I don't know a lot about this, but if it makes you feel any better, none of the rest of us feel that way about Keith. Kevin doesn't know what he's talking about. He's just jealous, like he always is whenever anything good happens for Keith. Kevin's been competing against Keith since they were kids."

"Let's forget this ever happened, shall we?" she dabbed at her eyes and tried to smile.

"Sounds good to me. Here, let me help you with this thing."

Keith was laughing at them as they came out onto the deck. Phil, 6 foot 5, closer to 300 than 200lbs., was holding the baby carrier next to Mary, who looked little indeed. "Careful, don't step on her! You'll squish her!"

"Hey, it's you needs to worry about squishing her, little brother," Phil said, with a significant grin at Keith.

They left the baby with Brenda, and danced together for the first time in over a year. "This is something else I missed, " Keith said. " A lot of Saturday nights I wondered what you were doing."

"Not much," she admitted. "Got a lot of work done, though."

"I really like this—don't hafta try to be polite anymore," he said as one hand drifted below her waist and he pulled her closer. "It was damn hard to do sometimes. You feel so good."

Mary noticed as they went around the dance floor, that the other four brothers had all disappeared, and wondered what they were up to. She could only see Brenda and Bobbie sitting together. She hoped it didn't have anything to do with the incident with Kevin. She didn't want Keith to know about that.

"I know," he said. "You're really a meadow sprite, and the head pixies sent you to me to teach me how to have fun again."

She responded with that marvelous laugh she had that so warmed his heart. It bubbled up inside her, and he felt rather than heard it. She relaxed then, in Keith's arms, but couldn't suppress a yawn.

"Tired, Bro?" he asked. "We can go home any time you want."

"Not yet, we're having a good time. We need one."

They were hardly moving on the dance floor, swaying to the music, unaware they were being fondly observed by Jean and Pete.

"Am I mistaken, or does that girl worship the ground our boy walks on?" he said to Jean.

"Sure as I'm standing here," Jean replied.

"He is so lucky he didn't lose her. They remind me of somebody else we know." She looked up at her husband and smiled. "Remember, we used to dance just like that?"

"On the beach, to the car radio. Just you and me, before Phil came around." He kissed her cheek tenderly, and took her hand. "Think we can try it again?"

Keith and Mary were too absorbed in each other to notice, but everyone who was sitting this one out winked and smiled or nudged each other, seeing the younger and the older couples together on the dance floor, both couples so obviously in love. It was a charming, notable counterpoint—new love and mature, fulfilled love.

One by one the other brothers reappeared, all but Kevin. Presumably he had gone home as Phil suggested. Mary danced with Keith's brothers, Keith danced with his sisters-in-law, all of them taking turns at one point or another keeping an eye on Johnny, who didn't seem disturbed by the noise at all. Mary didn't know this was Keith's brothers' way of keeping an eye on him, and separated from Kevin.

"All of them at once in the same place is quite an experience isn't it? Whew!" Mary said as she sat next to Bobbie and Vickie, who were also taking a break. Keith was dancing with his mother, who had a few drinks and was trying to remember how to do the jitterbug.

"Tell me about it," Bobbie, who had also had a few drinks, said. "You can just kind of get lost, but your own husband is always the best one—isn't that right, Vickie?"

"Damn straight. And you notice how all the aunts and the cousins have to have at least one dance with one of them—the poor guys can hardly get out of bed the next day, they're so tired. They're too nice to say no to any of them!" she chuckled.

"And don't count on getting laid anytime soon, either. But Keith's younger, maybe he's got the stamina…" Bobbie said some other things Mary wasn't quite sure she heard right.

"Bobbie!" Vickie said. "You're embarrassing her."

"Hey, Mary, what was the joke, anyway?" Bobbie asked, shrugging off Vickie's warning.

"Oh, that—kinda dumb really, I just said Kirk had to marry a cop just to keep the women away!" she giggled.

"I thought it was cool," Vickie said, proud of herself.

"Yes, so do I," Bobbie chuckled. "Did you tell Brenda?"

Vickie nodded. "She said the rest of you aren't cops, but you're some pretty damn tough broads."

"I don't know about that, I'm not feeling too tough these days." Mary said.

"Honey, you'll get through it." Bobbie patted her hand. "Having a baby dumped in your lap like that can't be easy—and you volunteered! Don't know if I could've done that. At least I had nine months to get used to the idea. You're not alone, anyway, you've got Keith, and you've got the family. Don't be fooled by that pretty face, under all that he's tough as nails, I know he is. To get through what he has and come out of it in one piece is something all by itself."

"She's right, Mary—what?" Vickie looked up, confused.

Mary, shocked, saw Kevin moving slowly across the crowded dance floor toward Keith. The expression on his face told her he was up to no good. "Oh, my god," she said, and ran across the yard, with Vickie right behind her.

"What's going on, Mary?" Vickie asked, but there was no time for an answer as Mary tried to intercept Kevin.

She stepped in front of him, blocking his path, saying, "I don't think so, Kev."

Keith was unaware of the situation as he had his back to them, and was laughing and doing his best to keep his mother from falling as she wandered too close to the edge of the deck. The music was loud enough to cover any conversation more than a few feet away.

Kevin tried to ignore Mary, and when he saw she wasn't going to go away, he said, "So you're playing guard dog for the weenie now? Get out of my way, bitch." He raised a forearm to shove her aside.

Vickie came behind Mary, and grabbed his arm before it could make contact. She said quietly, "Kevin, what's your problem?"

"Got a fucking little bitch in my way, that's the problem." He shook off Vickie's hand, and used the other arm to push Mary aside. The force of the push sent Mary off-balance, falling against Kirk's broad back, as he came by, dancing with one of the cousins.

Kevin shoved Vickie aside and went for Keith, as Kirk turned around in surprise.

"Whoa! You OK, honey?" Kirk asked Mary, not realizing what was happening. He reached down to help Mary up, as Kevin was grabbing Keith by the collar and attempting to punch him in the face. Jean started to fall, and Pete appeared out of nowhere to catch her.

Keith and Kevin were yelling at each other, in a full-blown fistfight. The anger Keith had inside, unrevealed for so long took shape and exploded against Kevin, too drunk to be effective. Both men were furious for different reasons and were lashing out at each other and anyone else who got in the way. It took all three remaining brothers and Vickie too, to break it up.

Mary could only watch, bewildered, as the music stopped and the dance floor emptied. Brenda came up and led Mary back to where she'd been sitting with Bobbie, who was comforting the squalling Johnny.

"I think he's just scared," Bobbie said, handing him over to Mary.

Mary took the baby and tried hard not to cry herself.

"So what's that all about?" Brenda asked.

"Kevin was puttin' the moves on Mary earlier, and Phil made him knock it off," said Bobbie. "They thought they had it handled."

"I didn't tell Keith what was going on—god, what a mess." Mary sighed. The baby was settling down, feeling safe now with Mary. "I went out with Kevin a few times right after Keith got married."

She looked up at her new friends with tears in her eyes. "Big mistake. But I didn't know—"

"Oh, so that's what he meant when you came in. I didn't know about that." Brenda said. "It was a mistake, but you didn't know Kevin, really did you? Poor thing." She reached over and patted Mary's shoulder.

"He was trying to make more of it than it was. He had Keith half-convinced we had some big relationship going, and I hadn't seen him in months, in the first place, and I never slept with him." Mary shrugged.

Up on the dance floor, Vickie was patiently explaining to the combatants that if they didn't want to behave themselves, she'd be more than happy to lock them both up. Neither man was hurt badly, though Keith had reopened the wound on his hand. Kirk offered to drive Kevin home, which seemed like the best thing. At the moment, nobody really wanted Kevin around. A lot of the guests were leaving, it was late anyway.

Mary resisted the impulse to run back up on the deck and throw her arms around Keith. Let his brothers handle this one. She sat in her chair and rocked the baby, feeling responsible for causing the trouble.

As Kirk and Kevin left, Vickie came back down the lawn to sit with the women. Jean was right behind her.

"Are you OK, Jean?" Mary asked, worried, as Jean sat down.

"I'm fine dear, it's been awhile since I threw myself into Pete's arms," she said, laughing, trying to make light of it.

"Yeah, I think everybody's OK, " Vickie said, squeezing Mary's shoulder. "Kevin's going to feel bad in the morning, though, and Keith should have that hand looked at."

"Would anybody like some coffee?" Brenda asked. "I think I'm ready for one." Without waiting for an answer, she got up and headed for the house, with Bobbie following. Some of the relatives stopped to say good-bye to Jean on their way out, looking at Mary with curious eyes, too polite to ask questions.

The yard was empty now except for the men up on the deck and the women sitting at a table on the grass. There was a quiet moment where Mary was wondering if maybe she shouldn't just pack up the baby and get plane tickets for the three of them to someplace far away. New Zealand, maybe. Or Australia. Australia could be good, she knew people online in Australia.

Vickie interrupted her thoughts of flight. "Don't feel like it was your fault, Mary. It's not your fault Kevin's a jerk. But you should never have tried to handle it yourself. Kevin's a big guy, and you could have been hurt. He was too drunk to know what he was doing—according to Brian he's been at it since noon. I think we need to talk, you need to know some things, OK? And I don't want to discuss it here. Would you come by the shop Monday and talk to me?"

"Sure, Vickie. That would be a good idea…" Mary would gladly sit and talk with this woman she trusted, because she and Keith had long ago done the 'cocooning' Vickie had talked about earlier. Mary had no one else.

Later, during the ride home, both Keith and Mary were quiet. They were almost home when Keith said, "Bro, what happened with you and Kevin today?"

"He was being stupid. He was sitting in the kitchen, he grabbed my arm and said some rotten things. Phil caught him and told him to knock it off. I thought he left after that…"

"What did he say?"

"It's not important." It really wasn't as far as Mary was concerned.

"Mary, what did he say?" His voice was quiet, angry. Persistent.

"Why should I tell you something as trivial as that when you won't tell me the important things, like what the lawyer said about the divorce? Ask Kevin what he said when he sobers up." There, she said it. Maybe it was because she was tired and upset, but for the first time ever she was angry with Keith, and it hurt. Worse, she realized she was wondering if he trusted her at all. "We used to talk about things. You talked about taking time off to write before, and I encouraged you even then. And I need to know if you're getting a divorce, so I know where I stand. Do you realize Clarisse could walk into the apartment at any time and take Johnny? Wouldn't be a thing you or I could do about it, either. And I'm not just your good buddy across the hall anymore, but the way things are I'm just some chick shacked up with a married man."

Keith didn't answer.

They had arrived at the apartment building, and they parked the car, unloaded the baby and his paraphernalia, and went inside in silence. Mary put the baby to bed, and for the first time in a week, put on a nightgown before she went to bed.

Keith sat in the quiet living room, in the big chair by himself. After awhile Mary heard him go across the hall.

CHAPTER EIGHT

The place still reeked of Clarisse. Perfume, stale beer, and sex. He thought idly he'd never get his security deposit back, as he looked around at the stains on the walls. He remembered how curious Mary was—why on earth were there footprints on the wall there? Why were there all those holes in the bed? He'd avoided answering. Telling her would bring it all back, and he didn't want to think about it. In another week, the rent would be due again, and it would be time to get rid of Clarisse's stuff piled all over the bedroom. He'd left a message with her dad for her to come and get her stuff, but it was still here. He didn't know if he could stand to handle any of it, but he'd have to. It was bad enough to surreptitiously empty the drawer full of sex toys Clarisse had replaced into a garbage bag, and dump it when Mary wasn't looking.

He didn't want her to see those things that so deeply offended him. He wished there was some way he could get around having to tell her about any of it, but she already knew too much. Goddamn Internet. It would be so much easier if he could pretend none of it had ever happened, close the door and walk away and just be happy with Mary and John in a whole new life. But there she was, smack in the middle of it and it was worrying her that she didn't know. She had to have been so scared to actually snap at him like that. She had every right to know whether the man she was living with was getting a divorce like he said he would. If only he knew himself...

There was a roll of garbage bags left on the kitchen counter. He picked them up and went into the bedroom, and began stuffing Clarisse's clothes

in bags. At the bottom of one pile he found the wedding album. Like everything else, it had something spilled on it. Some of the pages were stuck together, but for some reason, he was compelled to open it and look inside, maybe to see one hint that anywhere, there was something good in the marriage at all. He found, to his disgust, Clarisse had taken a black marker and drawn horns and glasses, and exaggerated genitalia, childishly, on every picture of him and his family. On a few of the group photos, she'd blacked out everyone but herself in a clear heart shaped spot. It sickened him. He jammed the album into a bag with some of the cosmetic bottles and other things, tied the top, and threw it against the wall with such force he could hear glass tinkling from broken bottles.
Then he dropped to the floor, his head in his hands, and stared at the floor for a long time.

Across the hall in the big bed, Mary laid awake for over two hours, every few minutes looking up at the clock on the nightstand. It was after 2 a.m., and she had never felt so lonely in her life.

Finally, Keith came in. He went in the bathroom and showered, coming back in the bedroom after taking much longer than usual. He got into bed, neither of them saying a word. He sighed, sat up, and said, "Mare, you awake?"

"Yeah." She laid right where she was, with her back to him in the dark.

It took him a minute to get it out, but he said, "The lawyer laughed at me. Said it was the dumbest excuse for a divorce he'd ever heard. An excuse, Mare. That's what he said. He said if I couldn't handle a woman, he couldn't exactly see a court giving me custody of a child."

"Then the guy's an idiot. This is a no-fault state, and his personal opinion doesn't mean jack. We'll find another one." Her voice was firm, but cold.

He was quiet for a long time, looking at nothing, aimlessly fiddling with the edge of the blanket. "I don't know if I can do it, Bro. Sit in court in front of all those people and admit what a loser I am. There isn't any actual evidence of what she tried to do to Johnny, only my word against hers. You're right, she could just come in here and take him, anytime she wants. I've thought about that, too. All those what ifs--." His voice trailed away into nothing.

"In the first place, Bro, you are not a loser. Nobody thinks so."

"The school does."

"Well, fuck them." Mary sat up, angry now, but not at him. "You know you don't need the benefit of their opinion. People whose opinions matter, like Phil and Vickie and Bobbie, not to mention your parents, think you're a good, honorable man who's been through a terrible time. And you know Bobbie, she never says anything but what she thinks." She softened her tone a little, and put her hand on his knee. "And by the time it actually gets to court, maybe you'll feel better about yourself. All this stuff takes time. And we always have our ace in the hole. If it gets down to it and you find you can't do it, then we get out. I can do what I do anyplace at all, and so can you." Gently putting her arms around him, she rested her cheek on his shoulder. It seemed like she was always doing that lately. Still, it felt good to him.

"I've wondered what the hell I would've done if you hadn't opened your door that night. I didn't want to have to tell them then. You know, I was so, in shock, or something I couldn't think at all." In fact, he could hardly remember that night. He remembered screaming, noise, Clarisse bent over the baby with a pair of scissors in her hand. Leaping across the room, pushing her away. She was laughing, taunting him. She threw the scissors at him, and the next thing he knew he was standing out in the hall, wondering what the hell to do.

Mary was saying something. Back to the real world.

"I know. And it's true, like your dad said, you are doing a lot better. Little bits at a time are what we can manage. I'm no shrink, but I really think we can get through this. True, the biggest problem we ever had before is what to put on the pizza on Saturday night, but we trusted each other. I even trusted you not to look when we went skinny-dipping that time, because you said you wouldn't." She gave a small, deep chuckle.

"I lied. I looked." That was something he'd never forget. He should have taken her home and made love to her then, and none of this would have happened. He wanted to…

"I know you did. Didn't matter. Well, I did too, but then I never promised. I was horny for a week after that." Even in the dark, he knew she was blushing.

He yawned. "Damn, I'm tired." This would be the appropriate moment to make up for that missed opportunity, but somehow he didn't feel like it right now. He wondered why.

"Yeah, me too. Let's go to sleep, huh? Tomorrow's Sunday, we can talk all day if you want." This was fine with her. For some reason, she seemed happy to lie under the covers with his arms around her, and drift off to sleep.

Sunday morning Keith spent a long time on the phone with Kirk—or rather, Kirk, Brian and Phil, since the out-of-town brothers weren't leaving till the evening. Something was up, but Keith would tell her when he was ready. She hoped. They even watched some old movies on TV, Keith sitting on the couch, and Mary on the floor close by, like they used to. They took turns doing baby duty. In the afternoon, they went grocery shopping, which was something else they used to do together. They piled the bags around the baby in the back seat of Keith's car, and talked about someday having Kirk and Vickie over for dinner.

On the way home, Mary reached over, and (she thought), companionably rested her hand on Keith's thigh. He froze. "Please don't do that," he said in a choked voice.

"Oh! I'm sorry," she said, and meant it. She didn't ask, but moved her hand.

A few minutes later, he cleared his throat, and said, "Remember those long nails she used to have?"

"Yeah."

"She used to set her hand there, and then she'd reach down and squeeze. Hard. She thought it was hilarious. I thought it hurt." Another one of those bad memories that came out of nowhere.

"That's terrible, god—well, I won't do that anymore." She put her hand on the back of his neck. "How's that?"

He looked at her out of the corner of his eye. "That's OK." He might be able to relax with It.

"Good. Because I like touching you, it's reassuring."

"Reassuring?"

"Yeah, it's hard to explain, kind of—Keith's here, and the baby's in the back, and everything's fine. I don't know."

"H'm. Have to admit, it is nice."

"Just more stuff that people who love each other do."

"Remember when I first got the computer?" he chuckled. "You were so into telling me all about it, standing next to me while I was sitting down, right?"

"Yeah?"

"Almost every time you reached around me to use the mouse, I'd get a faceful of breast, if I turned my head just a fraction of an inch. And I don't know why, but it seemed like it was OK. Never seemed to bother you, either."

"And I'd kinda rest my hand on your shoulder—no big deal."

"We had no idea how good we had it, did we?"

"Not a clue."

With baby steps, they were moving forward.

On Monday, as promised Mary showed up at the police station. She went into the old, 60s style glass and steel building carrying the baby in 'the thing', and asked for Lt. Astor at the desk. That in itself was a little odd; not many people go to a police station just for a visit, and Mary couldn't recall having ever been there before. They knew Vickie was expecting her and directed Mary

upstairs to the Detective Division. She found
Vickie's office down the hallway from the elevator.

Vickie was on the phone; she directed Mary
to close the door and sit down. "You came!" she
said as if she was relieved about something,
hanging up the phone. She came out from around
the desk and sat in the other chair in front of the
desk in the cramped office. Smiling, she said,
"Guess the guys cleared up a lot of things
yesterday—it's really not like any of them to talk so
long on the phone."

Mystified, Mary could only shake her head.
"Keith hasn't said anything, so I couldn't really say
anything about that."

"He didn't? Oh--." Vickie sighed. "What are
we going to do with him. H'm—well. Maybe I'll
keep my mouth shut about that, then."

"It's OK, he'll get around to it sooner or
later. He finally told me about the lawyer, and I was
right, it didn't go well—the guy laughed at him.
Seems to me we could find another one."

"Yes, you will, Kirk knows some people,
that's part of what they were talking about."

"Well, that's good. He could've told me
that, though. It's so strange. He doesn't give me
good news like that, but yesterday in the car he gave
me a graphic description of something Clarisse used
to do him while he was driving. It was bad, too,
though I don't really—." She hesitated. She didn't
want to give Vickie the details.

"That's OK, the main thing is that he's
confiding in you. He probably feels like he's getting
some control back, or whatever. I'm sure you'll be
pleased when he finally breaks down and tells you
what's going on." She patted Mary on the knee.
"Keith still have his apartment?"

"The rent was paid up, so he thought he'd take some time to decide what to do. There's not much in there anymore, some of the things that were hers. Everything else we put in storage or at my place. He was afraid she might go in there and destroy his books. She already thrashed the computer monitor, and all those neat old family photos he used to have on the wall."

"Oh, what a shame about the pictures, but it's not a surprise, she didn't like us very much. Thought we were stuck up, I think," she gave Mary a rueful grin, and shrugged.

"Somehow that term doesn't seem to apply to anybody I've met—I think it was her."

"Possibly, possibly. So, I know you're staying at your place, have you considered moving? Might be a good idea."

"I think about it all the time. We need a bigger place, we've got his stuff and my stuff all jammed in there, plus all that baby stuff..."

"Stuff everywhere, I remember that! While we were building the house, we lived in a one-bedroom mobile home on the property, and there was stuff, all right! Almost two years we lived like that. That was one time I was glad we don't have any kids." Vickie nodded in agreement, remembering.

"Oh, yeah. We talked about having you and Kirk over for dinner one night, but we don't have a place for you to sit! I mean, it's not like I can't afford a bigger place. For me, it was fine, but those guys take up a lot of room, and not just in my heart, either!" Mary smiled, and tried to laugh.

"Do it, then. I want to try one of those great pizzas Keith used to rave about!"

"He did? Huh. That was nice of him." Mary didn't think their pizzas were *that* good.

Vickie reached over and picked up a small stack of business cards off her desk. "These have all my numbers. I'm giving you a bunch, so you can have them everywhere, bedroom, living room, car, purse, everywhere. If Clarisse shows up, you may not have time to go searching for a damn little card. She was arrested for drunk driving last night, so we know she's around. I'm usually in the office normal business hours. I don't care what time it is, I want to know, OK? Are we straight on that? I know it's probably tempting to kick her ass, or give her a piece of your mind, but don't do it. You don't need to be polite. She'd just as soon kill you too, no doubt, you've got her trophy."

"What a way to think of Keith! But I know what you mean." In a movement of unconscious protection, like Keith had done himself, Mary put her arms around the baby.

"I really don't mean to scare you, but we've got to be realistic. That's why I'm thinking it might help if you can move, just for the extra degree of peace of mind. It would buy some time, maybe. If she's not too persistent she might focus on something else for a while. Oh, there's tons more. I know this is an awful lot to comprehend at once, but I've been saving it up for months in case Keith decided to come to Kirk or me for help. There have been times I wanted to go over and cuff him and haul him home with us, I was so worried."

Mary smiled in agreement. "I almost went out with Kevin again to find out what was going on!" She told Vickie about the disquieting encounter in the lobby. She also told her about the note on her door the day Johnny was born. "But there are things he doesn't remember. He came over one day a few months after the wedding, and he told me enough things that I figured out what was really going on. But now he doesn't remember being there. Most people would've moved. I don't know why I didn't, but it didn't feel right."

"It's really a relief to me to know he's out of there. Both of them." Vickie gestured to the baby. "And he's got you to help him through it. You know there are so many men in the same situation. Most of them don't have the help and support that Keith does. Some of them don't have anybody at all they can turn to."

"Oh, I know, I was looking at a website and I sat there and cried for an hour. Not just because of Keith, but because of so many other guys and the real ugliness from people who are supposed to help, counselors and lawyers and whatnot."

"We haven't been much help, either, I'm afraid. The cops, I mean. A lot of times we arrest the wrong person, and sometimes we don't have any choice. But in this case, it's not going to happen, if I can help it!" Vickie sat forward in her chair. "Think you can stand some more?"

"H'm. I'm a tough broad, remember?"

"That you are. If you think Keith would go along with it, I know a guy he can talk to. This is a guy who's been through the same thing. Because he's been through a real trauma, he may start having some problems you don't know how to deal with. He might have trouble sleeping, nightmares, and even uh-sexual dysfunction. H'm, I'm kind of out of my depth on that one…"

"Like Bobbie said, it's too soon after the party to know." Mary shrugged and grinned, albeit sadly. "Besides, we had our first fight—well, argument, last night. We hardly raised our voices, but it was unsettling just the same."

"Oh, dear. Not about Kevin, I hope?"

"Kind of Kevin, kind of the things I need to know and he doesn't talk about, like the lawyer. But we got over it. God, I wish this would all be over so I could have Keith back!" she sighed, a tired, frustrated sigh. "This is not the way it's supposed to be. We talk a lot about how stupid we were, wondering why we didn't know how we really felt about each other until it was too late. And on top of it all, I keep wondering if I'm really nothing more than another controlling bitch because of all the things I seem to be doing—the money and all that." She held the baby close, sniffling and rocking.

Vickie went over and knelt by Mary's chair. She put an arm around her shoulders. "Honey, Keith needs your help right now, and there are times, I'm sure you know, that he doesn't know what to do. You're doing the best you can, and it's out of love, you're not getting any kicks from seeing him like this, are you?"

Mary shook her head, too upset to speak.

"I knew you weren't. I saw you two on the dance floor the other night, the way he holds you speaks volumes. It's like if he doesn't hold on tight, you'll vanish into thin air. And every time you mention his name your eyes light up. Somehow everything has gotten all turned inside out and backward for you, and it's not your fault. You should have your nights together to lay in bed and find out each other, but instead you've got 2 a.m. feedings and a man that seems almost afraid of you sometimes. But hold on, Mary, because this will be over some day, and I know you won't regret it."

Mary found her voice. "Thanks Vic," she managed.

"Hey, what are sisters for?" the phone rang, and Vickie went to answer it, which gave Mary time to collect herself. After a brief conversation, she hung up the phone and asked, "Are you alright?"

"Yeah, I'm fine."

"Oh, here's one more card. This is the guy I was talking about. Might not hurt to give him a call yourself. Well, I have to go downstairs, I'll walk down with you. Just remember, if you need to talk, you can always find me."

The two women went down in the elevator, and Vickie asked, "So, what about your family? Are they around here? "

"Nope, my parents are in Key West, living it up. I don't think they know the 60s are over." She chuckled. "And that's it for my family. No brothers, sisters, or any of that."

"At least you won't have any problem where to go for Christmas," Vickie chuckled. She stepped off the elevator, and waved as she went through a door.

The first thing Mary did after leaving the station was to stop at the mall and get two cellular phones. She had always thought they were silly, but in this case they might come in handy. Then she looked at a few apartment complexes. Location wasn't important anymore. She got brochures from all of them. By then, the baby was getting cranky, so she went home and tried to work, after feeding and diapering the baby.

Johnny was used to being home, and not being dragged around so many places. He was crabby and fussy and didn't know what he wanted. Finally, Mary gave up trying to work, and stretched out on the bed with baby, turned some soft classical music on the radio, and the two of them 'talked' for a while. She must have nodded off, because the next thing she knew, Keith was standing at the foot of the bed, grinning at them.

"I can tell the two of you had a high old time today," he said.

"Oh, sure, the excitement never stops," Mary said, her eyes bleary with sleep.

"Can I play?"

"Sure, sweetie, come on down!"

Keith lay down on the bed on the other side of the baby, struggling to wake up because he heard Daddy. He put a hand on the baby's chest. "Gosh, he's still so tiny…"

"You've got big hands, though—" she put her own small hand on top of Keith's. "See? Only he's gonna grow up and be as big as you, maybe even as big as Phil."

"Can't even imagine that right now."

"He's already almost twice as big as he was when he was born, did you know that?"

"You're taking good care of him." Keith ruffled her hair with the other hand, one of their old things. "Bro, can you help me do something?"

"Sure, what?"

"Think I can learn computer stuff in a year?"

"That depends on what kind of computer stuff you're talking about. You're not going to be an IT Manager in a year, but you could do all kinds of other things, I'm sure. What's this about?"

"Well, yesterday when I was talking to the guys, Brian said that if I can learn enough about computers to teach little old ladies and high school dropouts to use computers, I could work for him. That is, if you wouldn't mind living in Phoenix. But that's not right away. They agreed with you, I should take some time off and contemplate my navel, or whatever you said, because, hell—I don't really dare go anywhere until we know what the Bitch is going to do. They're lending me the money to survive on for a year. Anyway, I can't leave right away, till we get the divorce straightened out, and um--. Kirk's going to help me get a lawyer, by the way. But I wanted to know if you could help me figure out classes and things like that. There's no way I'm going out to the school. But there must be some other way."

"There is—lots of other ways, we'll have to find out what's available at the moment, but sure, no problem. And Phoenix would be a good place to be, eventually. I've been there, it's nice." She stretched and yawned. "Oh, boy, I didn't even get dinner started…"

"Hell, I don't care about that. At least, I've got something to plan for now. The future doesn't look quite so bleak."

Why did he have to pick this moment to tell her his good news when all she had for him was bad? Maybe not so bad, a bigger apartment would be a relief. It wasn't the apartment itself; it was the reason they were moving.

She tried to summon up some enthusiasm and bent over the baby, and kissed Keith. "It's good Bro. Would you feed John? I need to see what we've got for dinner."

Leaving Keith looking bewildered, she went into the kitchen and opened the refrigerator. She was staring inside not really seeing anything, when Keith came behind her. "What's the matter, don't you like the idea?"

"The idea's great, fine." She closed the door and turned to face him. "Clarisse has been arrested—drunk driving. Only, she's still floating around, probably stoned out of her mind, if she's got lots of money. So she got back from wherever it was."

"How'd you find out?" All of his previous excitement and good mood evaporated. Trying to sound matter-of-fact, not letting fear or frustration creep into her voice, she said, "I went to see Vickie today. She asked me to come by, and thought she was just going to chew me out for trying to handle Kevin myself. We need to move, to get away from here. One day Clarisse will remember about me, if she's forgotten, which I doubt, and she's going to come looking for you. Hell, she could move back in across the hall if she wanted to! Plus, your car is always in the parking lot, right where it always was. I don't know if she remembers, but she did see me get in my car and drive away one day. And it's usually my car that has the baby seat."

He sat down with the baby at the kitchen table, where Mary had left the apartment brochures and the cellular phones. "So that's what this stuff is all about. Shit. See what I meant? Just when you start to relax, she hits you again."

By now the baby was yelling for his own dinner. Mary had heated a bottle while she was trying collect her thoughts enough to recognize meal ingredients. She handed it to Keith. "We really do need a bigger place, though I think we should go for three bedrooms, because we'll have two computers running and we'll need office space."

"Damn, they're expensive." Keith said, looking at the ones he could see with his arms full.

"It's a tax write-off for the business, anyway. But it'll take awhile to get out of here. So that's why I got the phones. That way, if either one of us are out somewhere, we've got a quick way to call Vickie—or each other or whatever." She was taking some leftovers out of the freezer to put in the microwave. "So that's my brilliant news for the day. Sucks, doesn't it?"

Neither one of them paid attention to the dinner they ate; they looked through the brochures. Keith got a brief, humorless laugh out of one place called Astoria Square. Unfortunately, they didn't allow children. Only two out of all the complexes she'd visited allowed children. "I can't believe those people didn't tell me," Mary said, frustrated. "I mean it's not like we're planning on sending him away to boarding school, or something."

"I don't know, I guess we just have to pick one. Right now I really don't care."
"If we had more time, we could just say the hell with it, and buy a house. But a house takes too much time."

Keith got up from the table, groaning, rubbing his back. "Oh, damn, wish we could go down to the pool so you could give me a massage like you used to."

"This time of day, it'll be jammed," Mary said. "But you can still have a massage if you want, we could drape you over the foot of the bed. It's not like you're trying to sleep."

"Yeah you could, huh. Oh, I'm up for it, believe me. Every muscle in my body is screaming."

"Gee and we wonder why…"

She covered the bedspread with Keith's beach towel, saying, "There, you can pretend. Now, off with it—everything!"

"Everything?"

"Yes, everything. I used to stop about here," she indicated his waist. "But you've still got nine yards of legs and stuff."

"Stuff, huh? I wonder if I know what I'm getting myself in for here…" he chuckled, but dropped his clothes on the chair, and stretched out on the bed.

"If you fall asleep, I'll cover you up and quietly tiptoe away," she said, from the bathroom, looking for the massage oil. She came back in the room, and asked, "are you cold at all? I can warm this stuff up."

She knew the reason he didn't want to go down to the pool had nothing to do with the number of people there at the moment. He had never cared about that. His back, which used to have nothing more than a little bit of a tan at this time of year, was strewn with scars now, some of them from deep cuts that most likely needed stitches at the time, but never got them. As a result, they were ragged and ugly; red and white streaks and tiny round dots from punctures started at his shoulders and went all the way down to his knees.

Unconsciously, he tensed and jumped as she put both hands on the back of his neck.

"Don't know where that came from," he said, puzzled.

"Just relax, Bro, this is me," she murmured. "Imagine yourself on a beach with palm trees. I've even got a CD that's nothing but ocean waves, if you want to really get in the mood."

"Somehow I don't think that's necessary," he chuckled.

She remembered how smooth his skin had felt under her hands in other days. She knew the location of every muscle, where it connected with bone, every vertebra in his spine. Now there were odd bumps and dips everywhere; rough spots that had never been there before. Now, as she eased the muscles out of their tenseness, she had to resist the impulse to bend down and kiss every old wound in an irrational attempt to make them all go away. She wondered if he was regretting allowing her to so closely examine all this evidence of Clarisse's madness. She didn't ask; after all, maybe he wanted her to know, without having to look in her eyes and say the words, just how bad it had been. They were quiet, each of them busy with their own thoughts. The unspoken communication lay in Mary's loving hands as they moved over Keith's body, a stroke here, a bit of firm pressure there. She took her time; alone in her bedroom without neighbors watching, she could relax with the process.

When she was done, she used a towel to wipe off all the oil that didn't sink in.

Keith sighed, almost asleep, and said, "Geez, that was great, you're really good at this, you know. I'm surprised you never practiced. Why didn't you?"

Mary shrugged. "Guess I just fell in love with computers, and—between you and me, I discovered I didn't really want to get that up close and personal with total strangers."

"In a way that's nice. Funny—I thought I'd end up feeling really horny, but I don't."

"Nope, it's not supposed to do that. That's the difference between a trained massage technician and some chick playing 'rub the boyfriend'." She chuckled. "Now another time, I could make it different. But today you're not in the mood, really, and that's just fine with me."

"How do you know I'm not in the mood?" He rolled over onto his side, propping his head against his raised hand. His lifted eyebrow told her she was right.

She was sitting on the floor, looking up at him with a mischievous grin. "Didn't Kirk or anybody ever tell you? Bobbie told me."

"Bobbie!? What does she know about it?" Keith was surprised and embarrassed at the same time. He didn't know whether to laugh or what.

"Wait—wait, this is from the other night, OK? Aw, geez, don't look at me like that." Mary was giggling, put her forehead against the edge of the bed. "Um, Bobbie said after a party like that, I uh, shouldn't expect to get laid for a long time. She said—aw geez." Mary was so embarrassed! Giggling like a teenager, she didn't know what to do. "Well, Vickie said you guys end up having to dance with all the cousins and aunts and like that, and you're all too nice to say no to anybody. And then, Bobbie said, after a party like that, you've had so many strange boobs and crotches rubbed all over you, you can't stand to face another set!" Mary dissolved into giggles. She couldn't look at Keith at all.

"I always wondered what they were talking about. The three of them always hang together." He was chuckling. "I wouldn't put it quite that way, but you know, she might be right." He reached down and ruffled Mary's hair.

"It makes sense," she said, recovering her composure and sitting up. "Bobbie's been married the longest. And Vickie didn't disagree."

"So what do you talk about--do you guys sit there and decide who's the hottest hottie, or what? Now I've got a spy in the ranks, I want to know all!" He loved the idea that Mary had been embraced by his sisters-in-law.

"Oh, no, each of us thinks ours is the best. It's not even a point of discussion. And all of them—even your mom had that basic insecurity issue to deal with. They are really wonderful women, all of them. I never got any feeling at all that they were trying to put up with me, or anything like that. They never mentioned Clarisse once. Well, Vickie did, but that's what we were talking about at the time, just Vickie and me. I can't tell you how nice it is to sit with those ladies and talk. It's like they already know everything, and they're so happy to listen to what I have to say." Keith knew about her lack of family. They had talked about it often, which was why he took her to the party the first time, so she could see what a big family was like.

Keith sat up and put out a hand. "Come up here and sit with me," he said. She got up on the bed and sat next to him, an inch away as she'd always done, in the half-lotus she'd learned from her mother. This time Keith put his arm around her and let his hand fall on her thigh.

"Clarisse would hardly talk to them at all. Aunt Dottie was right, all she did was sit in a corner and bitch every time I moved two feet away. Like I was her fucking body servant or something. And she wasn't even pregnant yet! I was still, h'm-- enraptured, I guess is the word. She was beautiful, and chilly, and she made me feel like I should kiss her feet if she gave me the time of day. And I regret every second I took away from you to spend with her."

"You don't have to explain yourself to me, you know." Mary wrapped her arms around him, and closed her eyes. "You're not the first guy who ever got stuck on an exquisite creature and was almost lost himself. She made me feel like a grubby old bitch who does nothing all day but work. On a computer. Oh, yuck! But I'm your bud, friends to the end."

"Yeah, friends to the end. We still are, aren't we?"

"Friends, for sure, whatever else you want to call us. I don't know much about married people, because my parents were always into this 'open marriage' thing. But I see your brothers and their wives, and it is so amazing. I think that's why Bobbie, Brenda and Vickie always hang together. Nobody else could get it, at all."

"Don't I know it! So, what do you think, once all this mess is cleared up, would you like to officially have the name of a dead actress? I'm sorry about that, but Brian pointed that out the other day."

"Just like your kid went down on the Titanic. Musta been Clarisse. Anyway, you have to ask me right, Bro. Say those four words."

"All right, so I will." Grinning and laughing, stark naked, he sat down on the floor and folded his long legs into the same half-lotus as Mary. Sitting up perfectly straight, he lifted both palms. Extending them to Mary. He said, "Will you marry me?"

"Oh, yeah, honey. In a heartbeat."

She bent forward, started to kiss him, and he stopped her, with both hands lightly on either side of her face. "One word. You have to say it!"

"Well. Yes. How's that?"

"That'll do it!"

She bent forward a bit farther, and slid off the bed, landing on top of Keith, and they were both laughing. Johnny, not wanting to be left out of the family comedy, added his own commentary, so they were forced to regroup and something. Whatever.

This had to be their own celebration. To all intents and purposes, Keith was still married to Clarisse. It didn't matter how happy he was for the moment, there was no point in phoning all his brothers and his parents to tell them what they knew anyway. Keith and Mary were a couple. So now what.

What should've been the happiest night of their lives was transformed into something less than celebratory by a woman who wasn't even there. Mary wanted to kill her.

CHAPTER NINE

They agreed on Complex B after visiting both apartment complexes. They were nearly identical, but Complex B seemed to have fewer screaming parents hanging out doors. It wasn't any different from some kind of low-rent project at the time of day they visited, when a lot of the people were leaving for work or school. It was 'transitional housing,' where people lived for six months or a year while waiting for homes to be built, or a dozen other reasons.

"I'll never scream at Johnny like that," said Keith, as they were escorted to the second of two nearly identical apartments. Both places had the room they needed, and since it was only temporary, and they could move before the coming weekend, they took it.

Keith and Mary went home after the paperwork was signed. Mary signed as the sole lessee, since the less of a paper trail Keith had, the better. He had to stand there and watch as his 'significant other,' as the real estate agent kept calling Mary, signed on for a home he could never afford on his own. Even if he was working.

In other times, they would probably call Kevin and Kirk, rent a truck, and all of them would help move. Vickie would strain her back trying to move something too big, and Mary would flitter about, with the baby in the 'thing,' carrying small things and saying, 'be careful!' At the end of the day, they'd sit around and share pizza and some beers, and complain about what a bitch it was to move.

The way things were, Mary called a moving company who would appear early Friday morning, and be finished by Friday noon. Mary would sign a check, and that would be that. They couldn't risk having too many Astors too visible.

Somebody had used a car key to scrape obscenities in the paint of Mary's car on Monday night, as Keith and Mary were joking about being named after Titanic victims and dead actresses. Words like, 'whore' and ironically, 'baby killer' had appeared. It was unusual in this neighborhood where these kinds of things rarely happened. Clarisse was sending a message.

Thursday evening Keith came home from the store to find Mary sitting at the computer desk, with the keyboard set aside. There was something that almost looked like the baby 'thing'—all straps, on the desk on Mary's right.

The baby was in his bed in the other room, and Keith had no idea. "Whatcha doin', Bro?" he asked.

"Cleaning my gun," Mary said casually. She didn't look up to see Keith's stunned face. "So, did you find what you were looking for?"

"Jesus Christ," he gasped. "What the fuck? Why do you have a gun, for god's sake?" He reached over with a finger and picked up the 'thing'. He saw the bullets lying in a neat row, and the guts of the gun lying on the desk blotter.

"What the hell's this?"

"My shoulder holster." Finally, she turned around in the chair and looked at him. "Bro, I've had a gun forever. I never told you about it?"

He looked at her like he'd never seen her before. "You never told me a goddamn thing about any guns."

"It's not like I've got an arsenal or anything. Just this little 38." He didn't get it. "Honey, I used to live in Detroit. Downtown Detroit. Alone??? Huh? I've lived alone practically my whole life. I meant to ask Vickie the other day about concealed weapons permits here, but I forgot. I've got one for the State of Michigan, but it's such a royal pain anyway, I didn't think I'd have time."

"Time! For what?" He was staring at her like she'd sprouted another head.

"Uh—dontcha think I should be carrying? We got this bitch trying to kill us all? I mean, it's not like I don't know how to use it—I go down to the range every so often, to keep in practice. We're moving tomorrow, Bro, I can't just leave it in the drawer where it's been, anyway. I have to have it on me."

"I don't want that thing on you." He was angry with Mary, seriously angry.

"What?"

"I don't want that thing near my son, either." Keith's anger was mounting to a fury she'd never seen before. "Get that thing out of my house! I don't want it here! Get it out, or I'm gone!" This was the voice she'd heard through the walls during the bad time when he lived with Clarisse.

For the first time ever, she was afraid of Keith. She tried to say something. "OK, I'll take it over to Vickie tomorrow morning…"

"No!" He slapped her in the face with the holster with such force the straps stung her eyes. "Now. Get it out now, or you will never, ever see me again." He walked into the bedroom and slammed the door. The baby was screaming, frightened.

"Oh, Keith…" She didn't dare try and go in there.

She put the pieces of her gun, that she'd owned for a long time, and only wanted to use to protect Keith and the baby, into a plastic shopping bag. Mechanically, she found her shoes, keys, and purse, and went out to her car with the graffiti on the sides. She got in and drove for a long time. Finally, she found Kirk's house on the lake.

Things were different now there wasn't a party going on. She could drive all the way down to the end of the driveway, where both their cars were parked. It wasn't late, after all, maybe only 6 or 7 at night. She stopped the car, got out, and wondered what to do next. She felt like a fool, standing there with a plastic bag in her hand, but she honestly didn't know where to find the door to this architectural wonder.
All she could do was stand there and cry.

"Mary, what are you doing here?" Kirk was surprised, but not unkind. He was just coming up from the lake, dripping from a swim.

She turned around to speak to him, but he looked so much like Keith in the evening summer light, that all she could do was cry harder. "Is Vickie home?" she managed to squeak.

"Sure she is, honey, what's wrong?"

All Mary could do was cry. Carrying her silly plastic bag, she let Kirk guide her up the stairs to the kitchen where Vickie was cooking dinner.

Kirk tapped her on the shoulder, said softly, "Vic, she's got a torn down 38 in this bag. I have no idea what the hell it's all about. Would you help her, please? I'm gonna go call Keith."

Vickie was a woman first, then a cop. When she turned and saw Mary in such anguish, she almost cried herself. "Oh, sweetie. Let me take that." She took the bag out of Mary's hand. "Come and sit down over here." She led Mary to the same kitchen table where she'd sat and shared jokes only days before.

"So what's with the gun?" Vickie asked, after she got Mary a glass of water and a handful of tissues.

Mary drank down almost all the water, then said, "I've had it forever, Vic. 10 years maybe? I go down to the range a few times a year, to make sure I'm not out of practice. I've got a concealed weapons permit for Michigan, but right now I didn't want to dick around with that. I thought I should be carrying it, with Clarisse on the loose." Mary stopped to blow her nose, and cry some more.

"Keith was so mad. He's never yelled at me before. Not like that. I thought he knew about it a long time ago, but I don't normally go around bragging about the piece in the bottom drawer, like some people do. So maybe it never got mentioned, I don't know." She sniffled, wiped her eyes, and drank some more water. Vickie refilled the glass. "But we're moving tomorrow. I couldn't just leave it in the drawer. I used to have it on me all the time, but here, I don't need it. But I figured, the way things are, I should start carrying it again. Seemed reasonable to me, but Keith lost it. I've got a shoulder holster, I think it's still in the car, and he slapped me with it ...he meant to hurt me!" Mary put her head down on the table and sobbed.

Vickie could do nothing for Mary but stroke her hair and wait. Kirk came back in the room and said, "I can't get him on the phone. He's either just not answering, or maybe he's on his way out here. What's goin' on, Vic?"

Vickie shrugged. "She owns a gun—that 38 over there in pieces. Has had it for a long time. For some reason, it scares the shit out of him. I couldn't tell you why, because she didn't threaten him with it. She knows what she's doing. Naturally enough, she took it out to clean it tonight, because she intended to start carrying it again, and they're moving tomorrow, anyway. You figure why it scared him enough to go off like that. He took her holster and deliberately slapped her in the face. This is not our brother Keith." She looked down at Mary crying her heart out. "I don't know what to tell you, honey, really I don't."

"He better not be turning into another Kevin, I'd hafta kick his ass." Kirk said, weary from family trouble.

"He's had his ass kicked plenty. We've talked about it before. Don't even think about it!" The warning look she gave her husband was enough.

"I know, honey, I'm sorry. Too bad she couldn't just take her little gun and blow the bitch away."

"That was my plan, you know." Mary sat up, making use of the tissues. "Shoot first, ask questions later. So what if they put me in jail? Wouldn't be long, anyway. First offense, self defense, all that happy horseshit. Brenda or somebody would help take care of John, and Keith would be safe."

Vickie said, "I'm looking at you, I've smelled your breath, and I know better, but I'd swear you were drunk the way you're talking."

"That's because you haven't seen him, Vic. You either, Kirk. He won't go down to the pool at the apartment anymore, even though it's 90 degrees and he always loved swimming. He doesn't want anybody to see him. He's got scars from here," she pointed to her knees, "to here" she pointed to her neck, "from the shit that bitch put him through. She used everything from forks to knives to scissors on that man. He couldn't fight back. He's got big strong hands and he could break her in two, but he didn't dare. Guess who'd go to jail then! She's said she was going to kill John even before he was born, and she keeps on trying." Mary took a deep breath. "He feels like shit because I'm paying the rent, and the place we're going is like some kind of weird yuppie 'projects' thing with all the parents screaming at their kids. Three grand a month to live in a freaking circus. All because the goddamn system won't believe a female can be a dangerous criminal."

"He didn't tell me much," Kirk started to say.

"You wouldn't believe me if I told you," Keith said, coming into the kitchen. He had the baby in the 'thing,' and he looked terrible.

Mary got up and moved to the other side of the table. She wasn't afraid anymore, with Kirk and Vickie right there, but she was angry and deeply disappointed. She couldn't say anything, not yet. She looked at him, her eyes swelled and red from crying, with a welt rising across her cheek where he'd hit her.

Nobody spoke. He slumped into the chair Mary had left, his eyes not leaving Mary's hurt face. Vickie, as the closest, gently reached over and took the baby out of the 'thing,' before Keith could squish him against the table edge. "I can't believe I did that to you," he said.

"And you'll never do it again. We never needed rules before, but now we've got one. Only one. Nobody hits anybody. Ever. If I do something you don't like, you tell me. Maybe that's the only way you could deal with Clarisse, but I'm not her. But if you ever hit me again, I will have to leave. I love you, Bro, but I can't be in a place where anybody will hurt me."

He had nothing to say for himself. He could only sit and stare at the damage he'd done. Kirk and Vickie moved to go out of the room, and leave them alone.

"Wait—." Keith said. "I want you to know why this happened." He put his elbows on the table, and dropped his face in his hands. His voice was muffled, but the words were clear. "She had a gun. A toy, almost. It was so small it fit in this garter thing she wore. She thought it was the coolest thing--. She used to come up next to me and hold it to my head, and say, "Pow!" So she could watch me jump. She kept the bullets in her purse, so I couldn't get at them. I never knew if it was loaded or not. Sometimes it was. She took all the pictures off the wall one night, and shot them. Lined them up on the bed next to me and she said she was 'getting rid of all that goddamn family'. The damn bed was full of holes."

"She hated us," Kirk said, not understanding why.

"There's nothing wrong with the family. You are all the kindest, most decent people I've ever known. She hated everybody else Keith knew," Mary said. "It was a general, all-purpose hate. Her own child--." Mary shuddered, and shook her head. "It wasn't only the Astors, or the people in the apartments, it was everybody. Not was, either. Is.

She's floating around out there somewhere, with all this hatred."

She walked around the table, and sat in the chair next to Keith, back in control of herself. "Bro, the other day I did something you didn't like. You told me so, and I won't do it anymore. Everything else is the same way. All you have to say is 'please don't do that', and whatever it is, I won't. Simple. I'm just feeling my way around, here. I can't know things unless you tell me. It's not like the old days when we could spend a whole day together and not say five words because we already knew what each other was thinking. You've been away, and everything's different now. You expect me to tell you what I need, don't you? I had no way of knowing you didn't want a gun around. It was there. I've had it a long time. What else can I say?" She was pleading, with her last reserves of energy.

He started to reach for her hand, and stopped. "Tell me you're not afraid of me."

She looked down at their hands, only inches away from each other on the table. It would be so easy to reach out, but she couldn't. Not yet. "There are a lot of things I'm afraid of right now, Bro, but you're not one of them. Anyway, what I'm feeling right now is far less important than what you're feeling. We have to put all our energy into taking care of you right now, and I know how much you despise that. You don't want to be the center of attention, but it's the way it is. Friends to the end, goddammit."

She sighed, tired, looked around the kitchen, noticed Vickie and Kirk had discreetly withdrawn, taking Johnny with them. "I've got so much yet to do tonight. The movers are coming at 7:30. Can we go home now?" Her voice was plaintive, and she had no more to say.

CHAPTER TEN

The move went smoothly, quickly. It was easier than Mary had even imagined. Even with the collections of two combined households, the new place looked empty. There were three bedrooms, two bathrooms, with a full-sized kitchen, breakfast area and dining room. One bedroom was dubbed 'the office,' with two computers and Mary's filing cabinets. Mary's couch and the Daddy chair looked rather foolish in the big living room, and the bassinette and dresser all by themselves in the baby's room looked lonely indeed. They needed curtains, shades, more bookcases. Mary spent the afternoon taking measurements, and deciding what she wanted, looking at furniture online. She ordered a new monitor for Keith's computer, and a real office chair for him, since he'd been using a kitchen chair at his apartment. She suspected he hadn't even turned on his computer in months.

The next morning, which was Saturday, they took Mary's car in for repainting, and stopped along the way at the storage locker for such small things of Keith's as would fit in one car. All he really wanted were his books, and his clothes that wouldn't fit in the closet at Mary's old place. The bigger things held too many bad memories.

"You know, we could fit a pool table in here," Keith joked, as he stood in the empty dining room.

"Or a gym—you could teach Johnny to lift weights," Mary chuckled.

"Speaking of whom, do you think he's OK in there all by himself? It feels funny not having him in with us anymore."

"I don't know, he seems all right to me, but then it's only been one night. We can move him back, if you want." She wrapped her arms around his waist and looked up at him. "Someday he will definitely need his own room, but for now, I don't see why not."

"Yeah. I kept waking up, and I didn't know where he was once—kind of a strange feeling."

"Yeah, I heard you prowling around last night."

"I try to be quiet..." He didn't think she knew he was still doing that.

"You are quiet, it's OK, Bro. Anyway, if we move him back in with us, it'll give us room in there to decorate. H'm—if you lose any more weight, you're gonna blow away in a stiff breeze."

"Haven't had much appetite lately." He put his arms around her and pulled her closer. "You, on the other hand, appear to be going the other way."

"A little water retention, maybe, my clothes still fit."

"Looks good on you."

"How do you know, you're not looking."

"Yeah, I am."

"You got eyes in your hands?"

Keith answered with a deep chuckle, and slid both hands under the elastic of her slacks.

Mary said, "I have to ask you something."

"What." His mind was not on further discussion of anything.

"That time at the old place, the time you don't remember?"

"Yeah?"

"I was just wondering if you ever figured out why."

"H'm. I don't know—it's kind of, it was just you and me and that white sweater and those tight jeans. I used to think about that white sweater a lot. Definitely an irresistible impulse."

Mary was quiet.

"God, are you mad at me now?"

"No," she said slowly. "Only I don't have a white sweater, and I know I wasn't wearing jeans. I hardly ever wear jeans any more. Now I wonder what that's about. You remember everything—well, you did before."

"I do have trouble sometimes," he admitted. "But that one really bothers me. I used to picture you in that white sweater all the time, and now I don't know where it came from."

That night, they were lying in bed, both of them surprised at how quiet it was now. They had dreaded the possibility of teenagers and hip-hop music next door, or on the lower floor. But it looked like this place was going to work out all right.

"Bro?" Asked Keith, softly in the dark.

"H'm?"

"You okay from that stunt I pulled the other day?"

"I think so. But I think--."

"What?"

"I think you need to do some counseling or something. Because that wasn't you there that night, it was somebody I used to hear through the wall. That crap is not going to spill over on me. It's bad enough worrying about Clarisse, I'm not going to worry about you too."

"Yeah. I'll do it. I've been thinking about it a lot. I don't want to lose you again, and definitely not from something that stupid."

They had crossed an invisible line somehow. Keith had done something the 'old' Keith would never have done. Clarisse had caused damage that lingered on long after the physical injuries had healed. The lost memories, Keith's reaction to the gun unnerved Mary. The man she had known so well was only with her part of the time, and she wasn't sure how much more of Clarisse's influence was still buried somewhere in Keith, waiting to jump out at her when she least expected it.

They had long weeks of peace after that, taking turns with the baby, hanging curtains and making the place look like home. There was a lot happening. Once the new monitor and chair arrived, Mary had both computers up and running, and Keith would sit at his computer while Mary was working on hers. He'd sit and swear at it and argue with it, and sometimes Mary would get up and take a look at what he was doing. Then they'd both laugh at where Mary was standing, remembering. Mary was surprised to find that what had really been going through Keith's mind back at the old apartment was just to put his arm around her and bury his face in her breasts. For the first minute, anyway.

Keith met with both the counselor and the new lawyer in the same week. Of course, neither of them had any clear-cut answers for him, but it was a start. Keith was able to file for divorce and temporary custody of Johnny, and the counselor said Keith's strange memory problems was likely due to Post Traumatic Stress Disorder. A name for it was better than nothing. Both the lawyer and the therapist took Keith seriously.

They had a quiet evening going; Johnny was down for the night and both Keith and Mary were hard at work. Mary's desk was by the window, and Keith's was along the wall with the door on his right. The way they arranged the desks was a compromise because Keith hated working with his back to the room. At least this way he didn't have his back to the door, too. They both agreed when they bought a house in Arizona it would have a room big enough for both of them to have their desks exactly the way they wanted.

Mary was reading through a recent avalanche of submissions: most of which were badly-written, or so full of typos and spelling and grammar errors as to make them almost unreadable.

"I got your e-mail, honey, thanks." Keith said, looking at her out of the corner of his eye, and grinning.

"What e-mail? I haven't e-mailed you for days." Sometimes she'd send him jokes or silly notes.

"Yeah, you did, only you didn't know it was me."

"Wouldn't have been that one about going back to school over 30, would it?"

"That's the one."

"I wondered about that, it sounded like you. So you pulled a Stephen King and submitted it under another name just to see if you could." She chuckled. "It was the only decent thing I'd read in days. We couldn't not publish it." She shrugged. "I wonder why I always say we when it's just me...h'm. Anyway, when did you have time to do this?"

"I wrote it a long time ago—it was in the 'puter, and I never got around to sending it over." Back during the bad time. Neither of them needed to say that now.

Keith was working on his novel. Mary was used to odd questions coming from him out of the blue when he wanted a female opinion on something, but she wasn't ready for this one. "Mare, what do you think about when we're making love?"

"I lie still and think of England." She had no idea what else to say.

"Yeah, right, and I'm the Prime Minister. HA! Really, I want to know."

"I don't know—h'm. Depends upon when, I guess. Uh, early, or uh, later? Just me or women in general?"

"Just you. From the first minute." He'd stopped typing. He turned the chair around and was sitting there with his arms folded, watching her.

"Well, it's not the same every time, of course. And if you're looking for literate-sounding, articulate quotes forget it. Is this going in the book?"

"Nope, curious, is all."

"Oh, well, that's different." She stared at the computer screen for a minute. "Some women fantasize—movie stars, news anchors, that sort of thing. I don't need to. I'm very much in the moment, and very much with you."

"News anchors? Really?" He chuckled.

"Yeah, I forget where I heard that. I did try that fantasy thing with Eliot once because he was so, well, he didn't like sex much. Not with me anyway. But I started to giggle, and it made him mad."

"I can't imagine him not—"

"Lynn's a guy." She still wasn't looking at him. "Guess I was Eliot's exercise in straddling the fence. That last month or two was pretty bad. I'd always thought it was me, or that he had his head so far into computers he forgot how to be a person."

"How come you never told me he was gay?"

"Because I didn't want to believe it until— well, when you were gone, I had a lot of time to think about things. He tried to make me believe he was leaving me because it was somehow my fault. Anything as long as I didn't think he was gay. So when you and I sat at your place that time and talked all night, I still didn't know, didn't realize, whatever. Well!" She took a deep breath and looked over her shoulder, trying to smile at Keith. "This is not what you asked me about." She put her elbows on the desk, pushing the keyboard out of the way, and rested her forehead on her clasped hands.

"It's OK, Bro. Really. Maybe you've got something you need to say, so say it. You're not done yet." He slid his chair over next to hers and put his hand lightly on the back of her neck.

"Aw, geez, why'd you have to say that?"

"Say what?"

"I'm not done yet. You said that the day you don't remember right. Only then what I was thinking was something like, 'sure honey, let's have some more of that'! What a fine line it is—." She looked at him with sad eyes, and looked back at the gobbledygook on the computer screen.

"The white sweater you don't have? That day?"

She nodded. "When it was you, it was nice. I wanted it just as much as you did. It was a surprise, but...when it was Eliot, it was entirely different. I guess it was a last-ditch attempt to prove something to himself, or to me, I don't know. Anyway, he came charging into the kitchen like he was really pissed off about something—the whole thing only took about 30 seconds. He didn't even say anything, I started to say hello or something, because he was about four hours late, it was almost midnight. But he started tearing off my clothes and knocked me down on the floor and well—screwed me. That's all it was. Then he just left me lying there and went and stood in the shower for an hour—maybe longer. I went to bed. Like nothing happened. The next day he left." She said it with no emotion at all—like she was reading a grocery list.

Keith was rubbing her back. He stopped, and folded his hands in his lap. "He raped you. How badly were you hurt?" Not, 'were you hurt' but 'how badly were you hurt?' His voice was steady, his eyes calm.

Mary struggled to stay as calm as Keith was, but she was reliving the worst night of her life and wanted to scream and punch the wall. " I was sore for a few days, and I had some bruises on my arms, so I wore long sleeves for a while. But I kind of tried to pretend it didn't happen. I never thought of it as rape until I started analyzing everything, like Dad would. It was more like, Eliot behaving badly or something. This wasn't an attack by a stranger in an alley, it was Eliot."

Keith's voice was soft as he said, "...who was supposed to love you and therefore could not be considered to have raped you. And if you think of it as what it really is, then you have to admit something really horrible had happened to you. It's even worse if somebody else finds out because then you have to deal with it. You can't pretend it didn't happen, or was something less than it was, because they know. It's always there in their eyes. Worst of all is always wondering what's wrong with you that let it happen at all. Am I right?" For some unknown reason, he understood perfectly.

She nodded, her eyes beginning to fill with tears. "For the daughter of a shrink, I wasn't very smart."

He put his arms around her and hugged her. "We're not getting any more work done here tonight. Let's shut these things down and sit in the living room. We've got things to talk about, and I don't want to wake the baby."

Suddenly Keith seemed very large, very much in control. She had thought he would be furious when she finally broke down and told him about her last night with Eliot, if she ever told him at all. His detachment reminded her of her dad, the psychologist. Funny she should be thinking about Dad so much tonight.

He took her by the hand and they went into the living room to sit on the couch. Mary was snuggled up against Keith as if having as much of her body in contact with him would somehow make her feel better. It did. Her head had started to ache from hours of reading followed by the intense emotions she was trying to contain, and feeling his heart beating against her cheek relaxed her. The pain and the anger were dissipating.

He was quiet for a long time, considering his words carefully before he said, "I told you about the handcuffs and things Clarisse kept in her drawer. The reason I hated them so much was because she used them on me. It was before she started getting too sick to go out. One night she put something in my food to knock me out, and when I was in bed, she handcuffed me to the bed and when I came to, she was shoving a vibrator up my ass. I couldn't see much of anything, but it seemed like the way she was holding it, she was pretending to fuck me and getting off on it. All I could do was lay there and take it. For a couple of days, I couldn't even go to work. Of course she loved it, I was there to be her slave, even though I could hardly walk. You were lucky; at least Eliot left right away. But I know exactly what you're saying, Bro, you wonder why you were so stupid as to let something like that happen. Only, there wasn't anything you could have done. When you live with somebody, you can't know they'd do something like that. And you do try and tell yourself it wasn't so bad. I did that with just about everything she did to me."

"Just what we needed—something else in common." There was nothing funny in her laugh. "It's amazing to me that after what she did to you you'd want to be around women at all." They weren't looking at each other; they were both looking at the turned-off TV and the bookcase.

"Yeah, Aaron, the therapist said the same thing. I guess some guys are like that. But she's the only really rotten bitch I've ever known. Wendy was irritating as hell, but she wasn't evil. She probably married some guy that thinks all that weird stuff she does is cute. Anyway, I could say the same about you—you could be a real rabid man-hater, but you're not. I haven't exactly been an angelic presence either, but you still love me."

"I think I always have loved you in some kind of misshapen way. But, I couldn't just start hating men entirely. It was only Eliot that hurt me, not all of them. There are still plenty of good guys around."

They sat on the couch and held each other for a long time after that. Neither of them spoke; it was almost like their old communication was coming back. There wasn't anything more they could say right then anyway.

CHAPTER ELEVEN

The next morning Mary awoke to look at the clock, and see that it was 8:30—later than she'd slept in a long time. The bed next to her and the bassinette were both empty. She got up and found Keith and the baby in the living room, sound asleep in the recliner, with the TV on. She tiptoed out of the room. Making herself a cup of instant coffee, using the hot water in the bathroom, she went into the office to check her e-mail.

A few minutes later Keith appeared at the door, with the baby in his arms. He had an odd look on his face. "Can you take him, Bro? We're both soaking wet—I need a shower. Yecch!"

She got up and took the wet baby, who was persistent in his morning announcements. She laughed. "You mean those diapers that are such a miracle of modern technology leaked! Oh, no! How long were you guys asleep out there, anyway?"

"Since about 1 o'clock. I couldn't sleep, and then he woke up, so I said what the hell, I'll just sit here and watch TV for awhile until he goes back to sleep. Guess we both went down for the count."

"Since 1, that's a long time for him! 'course that means he'll be up longer, but that's OK, isn't it, Johnny!" She took him into the now-decorated bedroom, and laid him down on the crib mattress to change him. Once he had a dry diaper and dry clothes, he was happy again. She pulled up the side of the bed, and wound up the mobile of stars and planets, which he liked watching and trying to reach. It was still new enough to keep his attention for a while. She went into the kitchen and made a real pot of coffee.

Keith came in wearing a towel, and said, "Oh, yes, coffee please!"

"So how was the chair for seven hours?" Mary asked, leaning against the counter, waiting for the coffeemaker to finish and smiling at Keith. "Surprisingly comfortable. You'd think I'd be a wreck, but I'm just fine. Wouldn't like to make a habit of it, though." He chuckled to himself and crossed the room to put his arms around her. "You're wearing that thing with the cats on it again. Think he'll be happy in there for a while?"
"Why, sure. What about the thing with the cats?"
"Can see right through it. Coffee's gonna hafta wait," he murmured against her hair.

Later, Keith was pouring coffee, when he said, "You know we don't do that enough. You're not, um nervous about it, are you, like uh, afraid of me or anything?" He handed her the steaming cup and sat at the table with her.

"Oh, heavens no. I'm very clear on the difference between you and Eliot." She rested a hand lightly on his arm and looked into his troubled eyes. "It's been a long time, Bro."

"H'm, well…it always seems to be me that makes the first move."

"I know that. And have I ever said no?"
He shook his head.

"That's because I'm not likely to. But I'm not really sure what's OK with you, and what's not. I've already found out some things I thought were fairly ordinary upset you. I don't want to do anything to upset you, so I tell myself, 'hey, it's only sex', and just kind of let you take the lead. It's only been—two months since you got out of there, and I don't expect you to wake up one morning and suddenly be the same guy you were a year ago. A year in the seventh ring of hell isn't going to go away in a few weeks." She got up and put her arms around him. "I already consider myself extremely lucky to have been in the right place at the right time. I'm sure not going to complain about not getting laid enough!" she almost got a chuckle out of him.

They now had whole days when neither of them mentioned 'the bad time', Clarisse, or any of that. Jean and Vickie phoned every few days to see how things were going. Mary even got a call from Bobbie once, and both of them sat and laughed about how Bobbie was right about, well—you know.

They went shopping for a dining room table, and even had lunch out together. "You realize something?" Keith said. "This is an event of sorts-- the first time ever we've all been out together. Grocery shopping doesn't count."

"We could conceivably live our whole lives and never leave the apartment, you know. Just order everything online. Wait till he gets bigger, we might want to!" she chuckled, and Keith agreed.

Once the dining room had a table in it, they decided it was time to have Vickie and Kirk over for dinner, finally. Keith had thought it was strange all she wanted to put in the dining room was a table, and found out the reason for that the day the sideboard and china cabinet arrived, along with assorted boxes of all shapes and sizes.

"All of this belonged to my grandmother," Mary explained. "She died about ten years ago, and my mother said she'd 'turned her back on the bourgeoisie,' so I got the good stuff. Of course, Mom wasn't too proud to take the bourgeoisie's money, though, once we sold the house," she said with a knowing grin.

"These are real antiques, aren't they?" Keith asked, opening a door on the sideboard.

"Yes, they are. And in this box are some of the tablecloths and things to go with them. You'll get a kick out of this—" she opened a box and pulled out a linen napkin with the initials "M.A." and handed it to Keith. "Grandma's name was Margaret Anderlie."

"That's cool, Bro!" He grinned.

"Wait—there's more." She carefully opened a big, flattish box that was sitting on the table. Inside was a mahogany case, with a tiny brass clasp on the lid. "Now—check this out!" She opened the lid and took out a spoon. "The family silver, my dear." Like most of the other pieces in the box, it was engraved with the initial 'A'. "Now what do you think of that?"

"Wow—I don't think my mother's even got anything like this. Is the silver antique, too?" He was really impressed.

Mary nodded. "M'm hmm. Some of the linens are fairly new, though, because Grandma and Mom started a hope chest for Mom before she turned into a hippie. There were sheets and pillowcases—the whole nine yards, but I didn't keep any of that stuff. Mom donated it all to a homeless shelter. When it came to these things, though, I put my foot down. I knew Grandma wanted me to have them. That sideboard's been in the family since it was new, and the china cabinet and the silver are 80 or 100 years old."

"So do we use this, or put it away? This silver needs some serious polishing." He was looking at the silver, packed away for ten years.

"Use it, of course. Grandma said the best way to keep it nice was to use it for every occasion you can think of. And she did, too. Even when it was just the two of us at Christmas time, she always got out the good silver. This is my favorite thing, right here."

She pulled a small, 5X7 painting in a modest wooden frame from its wrapping material. It showed a horselike creature standing on the African plain, with zebras and giraffes in the background. "Now, can you tell me what this is?" she said, in a goofy imitation of Wendy, the kindergarten teacher.

Keith shrugged. "Damned if I know—some variety of zebra, maybe?"

"You're close. It's called a quagga. They've been extinct since about 1830-1840. Somebody—one of my grandma's cousins, I think, was an art student in England in the twenties, and copied this off a vase at the Duke of Wellington's house. But I always had it in my room at Grandma's. Dad said once when I was little, I thought all horses were quaggas. When we'd go to Grandma's in the summer, every time I'd see horses by the road, and I'd point and yell, 'quagga!' They thought it was hilarious, and never corrected me till I was like, 4." She was laughing. "I thought it would be nice to put it in Johnny's room."

"Oh, the things parents do to their children! These things really mean a lot to you, don't they? I haven't seen you this happy in a long time." Keith was glad to see her smiling, and so excited about sharing these things with him. He put an arm around her waist, kissed her on the forehead.

"I hadn't even thought about this stuff in a long time. I just remembered about the napkins this morning! Only we won't use them yet, there are plain ones in here somewhere. But—hey, we can show off for the relatives now, can't we? And the quagga has magical powers—it keeps those pesky closet monsters away!"

Vickie and Kirk were duly impressed when they showed up for dinner Saturday night. As Keith had said, Kirk said, "These are real antiques, aren't they?"

"The sideboard's 200 years old. It's a documented Duncan Phyfe—I've got the old receipt in the safety deposit box, and the label is still on the back. The family legend is that the Anderlies came over from England right around the turn of the 19th century, because the original guy didn't want to go to France and fight Napoleon—sort of an early-day draft dodger. The dish the asparagus is in was supposed to have belonged to his wife. I'm not sure about that, but I do know it's so old my grandfather remembered his grandfather saying he got it from his grandmother. I think. Too many generations in there." Mary grinned.

"You'll have to let Brenda come and look at Christmas time. She loves old things. She'll be in heaven!" Vickie remarked.

"She must love old things, she's got Brian!" Kirk grinned.

"That was original," Mary said dryly. "But maybe Brenda can help me figure out what to put in the china cabinet." She gestured toward the empty shelves.

"How about some china? I mean, it's only a stab in the dark, but—" Kirk teased her.

"So who made the rolls?" Vickie asked, looking at Kirk out of the corner of her eye, changing the subject. "They're excellent!"

"Keith did. I wouldn't let him near the hollandaise, but everything else was pretty much a joint project."

"I didn't know you could cook, Keith," said Kirk.

Keith shrugged. "It's like Mary says, you live alone long enough, you have to learn sometime. I can follow a recipe, but Mary actually knows what she's doing."

"I spent a lot of summers with Grandma when I was growing up" Mary explained. "My parents were usually off 'finding themselves', in Arizona or Stonehenge or someplace. There's not much for a little girl to do in upstate New York, out in the country with an old lady. So she taught me to 'cook, appreciate fine literature, and good music'. According to her those are the three things you can't live without."

"That sounds right to me," said Keith, who had heard the story before.

"It wasn't bad, except that all the other kids were listening to Kiss and Bob Seger, and all I had at home was the Greatest Hits of Vivaldi!" Mary laughed. "Mom used to call me Madame Curie…"

"Her mother wanted her to be a scientist or a doctor," Keith explained, buttering his third roll. "Her dad's a psychologist."

"My goodness!" said Vickie. "And you didn't do it…"

"No, we lived in Ann Arbor, that's where the University of Michigan is, and my dad knew some actual scientists. I didn't want to grow up and be like them. In those days, they were stoned out of their gourds half the time. I don't know how any of them got any actual work done. So I got my degree in journalism, with a minor in English Lit, wrote for the Detroit Times for a while, did some freelance work, that sort of thing." She noticed everybody had almost cleaned their plates. "Anybody ready for dessert?"

She went into the kitchen, and was slicing cake, when Kirk called from the other room, "So what's a thing like this sideboard worth?"

"I've got the whole mess insured for two-fifty." She brought in two plates, and set them down in front of Kirk and Vickie.

"Two hundred and fifty dollars? That can't be enough." Keith said.

She was going back into the kitchen. "Oh, no, two hundred and fifty thousand." She said it casually, like everybody had $250,000 worth of dining room furniture, and she didn't notice the dead silence behind her. When she came back in the dining room with the rest of the cake, they were all staring at her.

"What?" she asked.

"Two-hundred-and-fifty-thousand-dollars?" Keith choked. "Is it really worth that much?"

"Well, prices fluctuate, but with the documentation on the sideboard, that's rare. Might only be worth a hundred, I figure better safe than sorry." She looked around her at the stunned faces. "What's wrong with everybody?"

"$250,000 is more than my house cost to build 20 years ago," Kirk said slowly, looking hard at the sideboard.

"If it's any consolation, I think they paid £20 for it when it was new," Mary chuckled, and dug in to her cake.

After dinner, everybody took turns holding the baby, and the four of them talked like they hadn't seen each other in years, rather than weeks.

Keith couldn't help bringing out what Mary called her 'family, such as it is,' album that had been packed away with the tablecloths. It consisted mainly of pictures of Mary and her grandmother, with a few scattered photos of her parents. When Mary protested, he said, "But you were such a pretty little girl before you turned into a hottie!"

"Geez, I can't very well say no to you now, huh?"

All the pictures were fifteen years old, and older, with the exception of one snapshot haphazardly stuck behind the last page. It was much more recent, and showed Mary standing by some trees with a sullen looking blond guy, who was not much taller than she was. "Who's that, Bro?" Keith asked.

"Oh, that's Eliot. I'm surprised that's still in there."

"Eliot, huh? That's him—the little shit."

"Who's Eliot?" Vickie asked.

"Software engineer," Keith said. "Dragged Mary all the way out here, and then dumped her."

"A week before the wedding. Maybe it was a good thing!" Mary said, smiling a warning at Keith.

Vickie looked at the picture, then looked up at Mary. Vickie then burst into laughter. It took a moment for Mary to catch on, but she did manage a little grin.

CHAPTER TWELVE

Mary and Keith liked to do their grocery shopping on Tuesday mornings, when the store was nearly empty. They went together, taking along the baby. Keith had his twice-weekly visits to the therapist; sometimes he'd meet Kirk for lunch afterward. A few times, Mary had lunch with Vickie and Jean, leaving the baby at home with Keith. Otherwise, the grocery store was their only outing.

This morning, rain was coming down in buckets and the weather had begun to turn cold, and they almost didn't go. But they were nearly out of everything including formula and diapers, so they decided to wrap up the baby and brave the perils. Later, they would wish they had stayed home.

Neither of them noticed the tall, blond woman in the pale blue raincoat. She was carrying a matching umbrella that obscured her face. They passed within feet of her at the entrance to the store, but they were concerned with getting inside as quickly as possible and keeping Johnny dry. Riding in 'the thing', and under Mary's raincoat, it would have been virtually impossible for any rain to penetrate, but that's the way new parents are.

They'd found only that morning they had gone separately to the same sale at the same store last fall to buy what turned out to be identical black raincoats. The only thing different about them was the size; Mary's of course, was much smaller. They joked about being FBI agents, and how Johnny was really an alien pod giving them telepathic directions. Keith moved a few yards away and called Mary on her cell. Silly stuff. Loving stuff.

Keith bent to kiss Mary, while giving 'the pod' a pat on the butt.

The woman in pale blue was watching. It was almost more than she could stand. She couldn't understand how that little slut with no tits ever got him away from her. It had to be that baby; that stinking, squalling monster that made her fat and gave her the gut that wouldn't go away. Her expensive tits were ruined, too, and now she wouldn't have the money to get them fixed for a while yet. Dad was already bitching about how much that 90-day rehab cost. All that crap about 'feeling good about yourself.' Well, it wasn't her idea. If they'd left her alone she coulda got rid of that baby. Now, he had the slut, too.

He was so goddamn stupid he probably couldn't figure out what to do with that monster, so the slut had to tell him. If he'd let her get rid of it in the first place, none of this woulda happened. She'd still have him. Right where she wanted him. Not that he was much good for anything; he wasn't any fun, but he was oh, so good to look at, and he had the biggest cock she'd ever seen in her life. Too bad he wouldn't share. With Kevin in her mouth and Keith down there, she could come soooo hard…But he belonged to her, goddammit! All her friends wanted him, too. They couldn't have him. Because he belonged to her.

The slut and Keith turned a corner and she couldn't see them anymore. She folded up her umbrella and followed at a discreet distance, watching them for a while.

Mary and Keith were at opposite ends of the aisle; he was trying to decide if he was gaining too much weight now he could eat again, and if potato chips would be a good idea. Mary was looking for rye bread without seeds. Johnny was starting to fuss a little bit. They were almost done anyway; they'd be home soon. "Hang on, Baby," she murmured. "Almost done here." She noticed a smell drifting in the air that reminded her of Keith's old apartment.

"He's mine, you know. Always will be," the voice behind her said. Mary turned around, not understanding. Clarisse. In the air around her were clouds of cologne, one of the elements of the odor that wouldn't go away in the old apartment. Mary noticed she hadn't lost any weight, but she was so tall the extra 20 lbs or so gave her an aura of substance that she hadn't had before. She was more like the Astor women. Her hair, clothes, and makeup were, as always, perfect. She was more beautiful than ever, except for her eyes. They were dark, ugly, and vicious.

In a panic, Mary put her arms around Johnny, who was escalating into a full-blown wail. She looked around frantically for Keith, but her view was blocked by a display of English muffins. She put the cart between herself and Clarisse, not knowing what else to do.

"Shut that thing up, or I'll shut it up for you. That you can have." She poked Johnny in the back with the point of her umbrella, startling him, making him howl louder, and laughed. "Where's my husband? I'm gettin' him back, you know. How long you think he's gonna want to hang out and play house with a midget slut like you?"

With trembling fingers, Mary reached in her pocket for the cellular, while backing away as far as she could, only a few inches. Everything was taking too long. She looked for a way to run, but she was trapped by the basket and a six-foot pile of bread. Suddenly, Clarisse backed away, turned and disappeared out of her line of sight. Mary fumbled for the phone, and dialed Keith's number.

"What's up, Bro?"

"She's here. I can't see her now—I'm still by the bread."

Mary didn't have to explain. Keith knew instantly. "Shit! Try to get away if you can."

Mary was peeking around the display. She couldn't see either Keith or Clarisse anywhere. "I don't see her—Keith, she's got an umbrella, and she poked John in the back with it."

"I can hear him. Go up to the front of the store, where there's people. Don't stay there. Stay on the line, honey. Tell me everything that's going on, and I'll find you."

Leaving the grocery cart, she headed for the front of the store. Mary looked around, but couldn't see Keith or Clarisse anywhere. She kept going, right past the cashiers, watching her talking on the phone, with one arm around Johnny. Slowly, she looked as far down as many aisles as she could. She couldn't see anything. "I've looked as best as I could, but I don't see her. I'm right by the front door, what do I do now?"

There was no sign of Clarisse, who seemed to have vanished into thin air. Keith, coming down the aisle looking confused, asked Mary, "What happened?"

"She--she poked John in the back with an umbrella. She was heading right for you—I was so scared!"

"I never even saw her at all. I turned around, and the cart was there, and you were gone. Oh, honey." He reached out and pulled them close.

At that point Mary more or less dissolved in Keith's arms. She was crying, the baby was crying.

Keith himself was so angry that here again, was something else he could do nothing about. They had no choice but to finish their grocery shopping.

In the parking lot, a nondescript blue car was parked a few rows away from Keith's car. The tinted windows hid the light blue raincoat, as the woman sat and waited. As Mary and Keith headed for home, the blue car followed, but was soon lost in the traffic and the rain.

Only moments after Mary and Keith drove into their 'security' apartment complex, the car came behind them. Because it was new, the driver blond and beautiful, the security guard didn't hesitate to let Clarisse into the parking lot. She parked in a visitor's space and watched them in the rearview mirror as they unloaded groceries, the baby, and went up to their apartment. Now Clarisse knew for sure where he lived. She hesitated. This rain was messing up her hair. Another day, once she had time to think. She started the engine and drove away.

Mary couldn't stop crying. She had never been so afraid, so terrorized before. She hated it. There was nothing at all she could do against this feeling of pure frustration. She kept going over the incident in her mind; it wouldn't go away. Clarisse's laugh as she walked away was almost inhuman. It was like Mary and the baby were inconsequential, worthless creatures, and they were getting in her way, like ants on a sidewalk. It was almost impossible to comprehend. She knew that Clarisse didn't love Keith, she wanted him the same way somebody else would want a house or a car. As Vickie had said once, Keith was a trophy.

She put away the groceries mechanically. Half of the things ended up in the wrong places.

Keith was walking with the baby, trying to calm him. If Johnny didn't settle down soon, Keith said, they'd take him to the Emergency Room so a doctor could look at him. To do that would be so risky. Keith must be terrified to even think of doing that. Mary could only nod, and cry some more. She was cold, and went into the bedroom to get a sweater.

In the bedroom, she found a sweater, and mixed up with her things in the drawer was an old bathing suit of Keith's. She sat on the edge of the bed looking at it, and remembered the day he had first appeared by the pool with Clarisse. They didn't see Mary; she was at the opposite end of the pool stretched out on a chaise lounge in the shade of the umbrella over one of the tables. It was the morning after a Saturday night, one of the first when the plant was moved. The two of them together looked perfect, her blond hair next to his dark, and they were almost the same height. Clarisse was wearing a silver bikini that left very little to the imagination--not the kind one wore in the water. Her figure was so perfect it couldn't possibly be real. Mary didn't understand what Keith was doing with a woman like that. She seemed not his type at all.

Mary was surprised at the horrible lurch her heart gave when she saw them kissing, touching. Clarisse slipped her hand in the front of Keith's bathing suit for a second, and pulled away. There was no one else at the pool, and they thought they were alone.

Clarisse's laugh reminded her of ice cubes tinkling in a glass. She lay down on a chaise lounge, in a classic pose, like something out of a magazine. Playboy. Hustler. She reached a hand between her legs and spread her knees. Keith was standing at the end of the chaise looking down. Mary heard him say something, and laugh. He turned and jumped in the pool, and Mary lay back, pretending to be asleep.

Mary felt like a very plain brown bird—a sparrow, or maybe a pigeon, by the same pond as a swan. She lay on the chaise, trying not to move, and was relieved when a few minutes later, Keith and Clarisse went back inside.

Keith gave a barbecue to introduce Clarisse to his friends the next week. Clarisse sat in a chair on the patio ignoring all the women; flirting with all the men. Kevin was the only brother that came, but he seemed to be the only male in the place unaffected by Clarisse's charms. Clarisse made it clear right away she wasn't happy to see Mary, so Keith stayed out on the patio. Mary spent the time when, in other days, she'd be helping with the grill, inside talking to Kevin, and had left early without saying goodbye.

Several weeks later, Keith saw her in the hallway and told her he was getting married. He was sorry, could not invite her to the wedding. Clarisse did not approve, and well--you know how it is, you want everything to go well…the look in his eyes said there was something not quite right there. But he was smiling, acting like he was excited. All Mary could do was wish him well, go inside and close the door. That day she booted up the computer and worked for twelve hours straight without a break.

Mary felt a hand on her shoulder. "Marc, hey, where'd you go?" Keith sat down next to her. At least she'd stopped crying, but she couldn't tell him.

Vickie came right behind him. "Mary, honey are you all right?"

"Yeah, I guess I'm OK. Kind of went off into deep space for awhile." She sighed, in an exhausted rush of air. She stood up, because she was afraid if Keith touched her again, she'd start crying. Seeing Vickie here only made it all worse.

"Vic says we should take John to the Emergency Room anyway, and it seems like a good idea to me."

"All right. I need to wash my face—I'm a mess."

"That's OK, there's no rush." Vickie said, as Mary went into the bathroom.

They were quiet all the way to the hospital. Maybe it wasn't smart, but Mary couldn't bring herself to put John in the car seat. She held him all the way. At the hospital, she had to explain to different people a dozen times that she was not the baby's birth mother. She knew nothing about the delivery, or what drugs or how much the mother had used in pregnancy. Keith had to answer those questions. She knew the name of the pediatrician, and that was all. So far, John had been fine—gaining weight and growing fast. Even Keith got a little tired of the probing questions.

"Do they think we did this?" Mary asked Vickie. "Don't they believe us?"

"They have to ask a lot of questions. In child abuse cases, if there's a stepparent, that's the first one they suspect. But don't worry, nobody's going to accuse you of anything."

Child abuse case—is this what Johnny was? "But nobody saw it happen—nobody but me, that is." Mary said, slowly. "Nobody even saw Clarisse at all."

"You're wrong there," Vickie said. "One of the cashiers saw her with an umbrella in her hand, talking to you in the aisle. That's something, at least. It's still unofficial, I'm just the worried auntie right now."

After x-rays, tests, and plenty of handling by assorted people, Johnny was pronounced fine. They could go home. "You look like you need some rest yourself," the doctor remarked, including both Keith and Mary in his glance, their names now cleared of suspicion of wrongdoing.

On the way home, Mary relaxed enough to put Johnny in the car seat.

"It wasn't just the thing with Clarisse, was it? There was something else, too." Keith said. "I don't think I've ever seen you that upset, Bro."

"H'm. It reminded me of something I didn't want to remember." This was all Mary would say.

The rain, relenting to a drizzle, was a perfect mirror of Mary's state of mind at the moment. It was shortly after noon, but dark as evening. And cold. Mary could not get warm. Back in the apartment, she put the baby in his bassinette, which she noticed he'd be growing out of soon. Then they'd have to put him in the big crib in his own room, and Keith would probably not sleep at all.

Neither one of them felt hungry, so Mary didn't bother to make lunch. She did pick up the grocery bags off the floor and throw them away. She made some coffee to take the chill off, and Keith went into the office to try and work a little. Mary didn't even bother to go in and check her e-mail. She drifted into the living room, lay down on the couch and surfed through radio stations trying to fit something to suit her mood. Nothing was really right so she turned the thing off. She lay on the couch, looking at the ceiling, listening to the sound of Keith's fingers on the keyboard. In the past few days he'd decided to work on the novel a bit more, and had made some progress.

She thought about a lot of things, lying there in the quiet living room, most of which revolved around finding a solution to their problem. There had to be something, because Mary feared Clarisse would get her way somehow. She could destroy them anyway without having done anything new. The old stuff was still hanging around, like the smell that clung to Keith's bits and pieces of furniture in the storage locker. Mary didn't know what the next days and weeks would be like; knowing Clarisse had caught up with them. How did she know where to find them, anyway? That question would bother her for a long time to come.

To think of the baby as a 'child abuse case' was not something she'd thought about before, anymore than she'd thought of Keith as an abused husband—not in those terms anyway. They weren't 'cases', any more than she was a wicked stepmother. Come to think of it, she wasn't even a stepmother, and she wondered why Vickie had used that term. Legally, she was nobody. She may even be a liability to Keith if Clarisse decided to fight the custody issue. Through no fault of her own, she'd landed in a mess of somebody else's making. Keith didn't deserve it any more than the baby did. Maybe it was time she stopped being afraid and started getting mad, but the fear was there. Fear of having done the wrong things, fear of waking up one morning and finding herself alone again. Johnny was getting more active every day, developing a personality, and they could swear they saw him smile and laugh, telling tiny baby jokes.

She didn't know what she would do if she discovered he and Keith were really only visiting for a while. She looked back on the time she'd tried so hard to forget Keith, pretend she didn't care. Would she have to do that again?

Some time later, Keith came in and covered Mary with the afghan that lay folded on the back of the couch. "Thanks, Bro," Mary murmured. "But I'm awake."

Keith started to go back into the office, and Mary said, "Don't go, I need a hug."
He came back, sat down on the couch, and wrapped his arms around her. At last, she was getting warm again. He said, "You had me worried there, Bro. Are you all right now?"

"Not really, but it was um—just stupid."

"Mare, nothing's stupid if it upsets you like that. Something you remembered, right?"

"Something I shouldn't have seen but did." She was quiet for a long time, feeling secure there for a moment with Keith. She wanted to cry, but she'd already cried enough for all three of them that morning. "The first time I saw Clarisse wasn't at that barbecue you had—it was about a week before, out by the pool." Mary continued, "There wasn't anybody else down by the pool, just me. You didn't see me right away, and I didn't say anything because I was trying to figure out who the chick was. Then all of a sudden, it was one of those situations where you just want to disappear into thin air. So I laid down and closed my eyes and pretended to be asleep, just in case you noticed me."

Keith remembered. "It was the first and only time she ever went near the pool. She wouldn't go in the water, but I did, and when I got out, she was laying there with nothing on. I was so embarrassed, well, mostly, but with four floors of apartments overlooking the pool, it didn't matter we thought nobody was right by the pool. I won't even tell you what she wanted to do. So you saw all that? Poor Bro." He sighed, and rubbed her back.

"No, actually, I closed my eyes the minute you went in the water. I thought sure you'd be doing laps and you'd see me when you got to my end of the pool. No, the thing that got to me was how—fascinated, completely taken you seemed with her." It was hard getting the words out. When they did, they came slowly. "I didn't know I would ever feel like that, I'd seen you with women before and never had that reaction. But it was like the world was coming to an end. I made myself forget it. I never thought about it at all till this morning, when I heard her laugh. It gave me the shivers. It made me wonder—does that fascination go away, or maybe one day will I look pretty damn boring?" Mary was clinging to him, her last words nearly inaudible.

"Boring? You? You've got to be kidding! I've never met anyone like you, Mare, and I mean it. You're always so interested, and interesting. Your whole life is an education, and I don't think I'll ever stop learning. H'm--but that's not what you're worried about is it?"

He answered his own question, with a little bit of his classroom manner creeping in. "No, what I think you're worried about, is that you've seen some statistics somewhere and you're worried if they apply to me. You probably know how many people go back to the person who abused them. Am I right?"

She let go of him and reluctantly sat back to meet his eyes. She noticed he had dark circles under his eyes, and today he was looking a lot like Brian, 15 years older.

"I hate to even think about it, but—"

"But nothing, Bro. I never loved her. I never even thought I did. I admit to being enraptured for a while, even obsessed, but…she was fun to play around with for about three weeks, then after that it got real nasty real fast. Sometimes I look around this place, and it's so comfortable, and you've done so much to make it into a home, I can hardly believe I got myself in that awful situation. I can hardly believe I ever thought you were a slob!" He shrugged, smiled, and reached out and stroked her cheek. "You're taking care of me in ways you don't even realize, because for you it's natural to care what I think, how I feel about something. You remind me sometimes, 'this is what people who care about each other do,' and I really need to hear that, because somehow in the last year I've forgotten a lot of those things, just out of necessity. For self-preservation." He stood up; picked up the end of the afghan he was sitting on and wrapped it around Mary. "Living with you is like coming out of a tunnel. All of a sudden there's light and air and quiet. I can hear myself think again. I know it's still back there, and it's not all that far away yet, but every time I wake up in the middle of the night all I have to do is reach out a hand and touch you, and I know I'm OK. Sometimes I can even go back to sleep." Keith sat down next to her, and took her hands. "I really, really, need you Bro. I don't love you just because it's convenient to have somebody help take care of my kid, I loved you anyway. For the first time in months I can even believe it's possible for us to have a future, without--. The guys that go back have long-term relationships, and they really do love the woman that's making their life miserable. That's one problem I don't have. I know she'll never change, and I honestly don't care what happens to her, even. Just so long as she leaves us alone."

"And how do we accomplish that, I wonder?" Mary said.

CHAPTER THIRTEEN

Aaron Rensellear looked more like a dressed-up auto mechanic than a therapist, in his jeans and denim shirt. He was also yet another big-and-tall in a world that seemed to Mary to be populated entirely by big-and-talls these days, she noticed wryly. His very short dark hair was going grey at the temples, the look of a retired military man.

Keith had asked her to come with him one day to meet Aaron, so there she was. As complex and strange as things were getting, she couldn't imagine what she could possibly add.

"Have a seat," he said, gesturing toward the couch, and she and Keith sat down. Both of them felt a little uneasy without the baby along. They'd left him with Jean this time. Aaron sat in a chair across the coffee table from the couch. "So you're Mary," he said, almost to himself. "So, how did you ever manage to get yourself involved in all this?"

"Right place at the right time, I guess." She shrugged. "We were good buddies, he needed help, I was there to offer."

"Just like that?"

"Pretty much—I don't remember thinking about it for more than a few minutes. It didn't seem like that big a deal. Things didn't get complicated until later." She looked at Keith out of the corner of her eye and grinned.

"But you're still here, I see…" Aaron said, watching her. "Things are a lot different now than before."

"Sure they are. Before, it was just me and Keith hanging out by the pool or whatever. Not a problem in the world, really. We always had a good time together, for the first few months we were both getting over being dumped, and it was easier just to be friends. At least that's what we thought we were doing, only in retrospect it looks rather different…" she reached for Keith's hand, and they shared a knowing smile.

"Did you talk about things back then? Feelings, for example?"

Mary thought a moment, framing her words. "I'd almost forgotten, but a few months after Keith moved in, we were sitting in his living room, talking about how rotten it felt to be dumped, mostly. It was a major crying-on-each-other's-shoulders kind of thing. Then one of us noticed a weird light outside, and we went to look, and it was the sun coming up. We talked all night and didn't know it!" she laughed at the fond memory.

"I remember that," Keith said. "Wendy left me feeling like, um, what was that I said, Bro?"

"Like you'd been expelled from kindergarten," Mary said, squeezing his hand, chuckling.

"She was a kindergarten teacher, and that's the way she treated everybody," Keith explained to Aaron. "Geez, that voice!" He shuddered.

"And Eliot was like a walking computer," Mary put in. "I think we both agreed eventually we were better off, but at the time--." She shrugged. "But we did, we talked a lot about everything back then."

"How is it different now?" Aaron asked Mary.

She let go of Keith's hand, and sat forward, with her hands clasped in front of her. "Some things, I know—he doesn't want to talk about. I get that. But other things, well, there were sometimes important things I needed to know and I didn't. It's frustrating. That's what our first argument was about. I tell myself that it's not a permanent situation, because Keith was always a lot more forthcoming than other men I've known. It's already improving a lot, so maybe one day we'll have that old communication thing back."

"You know I'm trying," Keith said softly.

"Yes, I do know, honey, but—he was asking." She turned around and smiled at him. It really was OK.

"So, do you know much about his family?" Aaron was asking again.

Mary snickered. "You don't know Keith without knowing the family. Well, Clarisse didn't, but that was her problem. They've pretty much all been a big help. Except for Kevin, but I guess every family has its black sheep. I know what you're asking, am I aware of any kind of abuse going on there, am I right?"

Aaron chuckled, nodding.

"Not a thing that I've noticed. And I think that the reason Keith was able to get out when he did, relatively early, speaks to the fact that he's lived in a comfortable, safe environment before and knows what it's like. If you want my opinion." She grinned at Aaron. There was compassion in her voice as she continued. "I've done some reading—there's not much, but of what there is I know some of these guys hang on for years and years. Their own families refuse to believe there's anything wrong, or else they don't even know because the guy isn't talking. All they know is the guy's wife is a bitch, so they stay away."

Mary sighed, and looking at Aaron with tears in her eyes, she said, "That's the usual family. The Astors are not your usual family. So, even if I hadn't been there, the family would've been. Vickie knew what was going on, anyway, from the very beginning, almost before Keith did--."

"She did?" Keith asked, mystified. "How?"

"Vickie's been surrounded by men her whole life. Her mother died when she was little, and she's got brothers of her own. Then at the police academy, I think she was one of only two women in the class. So she knows very well that men aren't pigs. And women aren't all sugar and spice, either. Plus, she's been a cop for a long time. So when Clarisse showed up at the birthday party, and put on her stupid 'queen act', she wondered what was up, because she recognized the signs. She never said anything to anybody, not even Kirk, but her radar was up, Bro. Why do you think she paid such close attention to me, at first? She wanted to make sure I wasn't the same as Clarisse!"

"That doesn't bother you, knowing you're being observed?" Aaron asked, with a raised eyebrow.

She shook her head. "Not at all. Keith's family has every right to know what kind of person I am. And besides, it doesn't feel that way. Being observed, that is. It's more like, Vickie's taking an interest. She adores Johnny, so we stop by the shop every so often just so she can see him. It's actually kind of nice. I don't have any family to speak of, my parents are in Key West partying hearty—I haven't actually seen them for ten years, but we e-mail, and phone once in a while. No brothers or sisters, so this is a whole new thing for me. If Johnny was actually mine, my mother wouldn't be offering to babysit and give me advice like Jean does. She'd send me a note and a check and that would be it."

Aaron looked at his watch. "Well, Keith, if we want to get to you we'd best be moving along. Mary, would you mind waiting out there for a bit?"

"Nope, I'll be thinking of lunch!" She patted Keith's knee and went out to the waiting room.

"This is our first time out without the baby," Keith explained. "It feels really strange."

Aaron smiled and nodded. "Speaking of the baby, how's the divorce going? Any custody problems?"

"Not last I heard. She hasn't even filed to contest the divorce. But she's not done with me yet." Keith exhaled in a rush of air, looking down at his hands. "She showed up in the grocery store the other day and attacked the baby. Mary was scared to death. I never even saw her. We thought we were OK after we moved, but somehow she found out where we were. So now it's back to looking over our shoulders all the time. They treated us like shit at the hospital. Like we'd hurt our own baby. Good thing Vic was with us, it would've been worse." He shrugged, shook his head. "Just when we were starting to think things might work out. I've got my appetite back; I've been sleeping better. Mary has been more relaxed, even. For a while it was like she was trying to be Supermom or something, and she's got a business to run. Now, it's like right back where we started, and Mary's somehow got the notion I might go back to Clarisse. Don't know where that came from."

"Have you talked to her about it?"

"A little. But I think this is something I could talk about till Doomsday and it wouldn't have any effect. I think it has to do with the fact that Clarisse was probably cleaned up, and maybe she had her hair done. Her dad won't let her get too dirty, he'd put her in the shower himself, if he had to." Aaron knew all about Clarisse's relationship with her dad. "But Mary feels, kind of , not quite 'up to snuff' around Clarisse, like she's not pretty enough for me somehow."

"But she's a beautiful woman!" Aaron protested.

"I know that. I think that might be Eliot's doing—the guy before me. He hardly noticed her, and I think that made her think she wasn't worth paying attention to, not to mention the fact that he raped her the night before he moved out. But it was a long time ago, and I think she's dealt with that part of it. I take a lot of time trying to convince her Eliot was wrong."

"And that's the fun part!" Aaron grinned.

Keith nodded. "Best way to convince her is to show her," he chuckled.

Keith and Mary were outside the office building, in the parking lot, trying to decide what to do with their free afternoon. "You know what I'd really like to do?" Mary asked.

"What's that?"

She shrugged and looked up at him, with a mischievous grin. "Let's just go home," she said.

"I hear that. We've got till four o'clock," he said.

"Really? Ooh…"

At 3:15 they were at home lying in their bed, enjoying the sweet afterglow, Keith curled around Mary like two puzzle pieces locked together. It was so quiet Mary could hear the ticking of the kitchen clock.

Eventually Keith said, "Mare, can I ask you something?" His voice had that near-casual tone that told her it was an important question. He'd been trying not to call her 'Bro', especially before or after sex, because it didn't seem, well, appropriate anymore.

She was just able to talk now. Her voice was husky as she said, "Honey, if you think I can give you a straight answer to anything right now, after the best sex I've ever had in my life, you can forget it!"

"You thought so?" he was pleased, maybe a little surprised.

"Oh, yeah. You've stopped being so careful with me," she chuckled, teasing. "For one thing." There had been times she was tempted to tap him on the shoulder and say, 'Hey, I'm not gonna break!' But she never did, and wasn't going to tell him that now. She wriggled around so she could look up at him. She saw his deep brown eyes had a glint of gold she'd only seen once before. It didn't last long, but seeing it was almost like another orgasm.

He saw her eyes widen in surprise, the sharp intake of breath that was almost a moan. "Wow, where'd that come from?" he asked.

"I could never explain that in a million years," she giggled.

"A chick thing?" His slow smile told her he understood. He gently brushed the hair out of her eyes. "Plenty of time to talk later."

"Hmmm. You know we never did have lunch."

They hadn't stopped for lunch, or anything else. They barely made it inside their front door. Keith had picked her up, a degree less than mindful, and carried her to the dining room table. They knocked over Grandma Anderlie's crystal vase and it had rolled harmlessly onto the carpet. It was out of the periphery of their consciousness; they'd find it later and wonder how they did that!

Keith stretched, yawning. "I know, I'm starving."

Mary sat up and looked at the clock. "We'd better get a move on, time to get Johnny."

"Yes, you know what Mom said when I called her last week?" He was laughing, suddenly remembering something.

"Huh?"

"She said, now don't you two fall asleep and make us late! They got someplace they have to be at 5. I just said, sure, Ma—I had no idea what she was talking about. Then."

"Oh, no! How come she always knows everything before we do, it's not fair!" Mary covered her face with both hands in mock frustration. "And now I gotta go over there! Yikes!" She grabbed a pillow and buried her face in it. "I think I finally will die of embarrassment. She's probably been on the phone to Bobbie and Brenda and everybody!"

"Aw, geez, honey, it's not that bad is it?" He was laughing at her. He leaned over and kissed the back of her neck. He knew how the family talked. "How's this—I'll go get him, and you can stay here and make lunch. Would that make you feel better?" She raised her head out of the pillow. "Yes. Definitely."

"OK—not a problem."

He stood up and stretched, and headed for the shower, with Mary watching him over the lace edging of the pillow. How close to perfect can somebody be? She wondered. God, he's gorgeous. She could allow herself these thoughts now. There had been a time when she didn't dare.

After that, Mary put some burger in the microwave to thaw, and had a nice, hot bath before Keith came back with the baby, wide awake and ready to play. She put the dining room, office and bedroom back they way they'd been before Mary and Keith trashed everything, smiling fondly to herself the whole time. Keith had the radio on, and was dancing with the baby in the living room.

When they were finishing their lunch, (more like dinner by now) with the baby in the high chair, Mary asked Keith, "So what was it you wanted to ask me before?"

Keith had given Johnny a strand of spaghetti to play with, and was watching what he did with it. "H'm, I had it all phrased, now I don't quite remember—well, it's something like, do you have what you need from me? Sometimes it seems like, I wonder if, maybe you're not getting enough attention or something." he sat back in his chair, and put his fork down. It was important. She could see he was having trouble asking.

"Keith, living with you is immensely gratifying. And it's not just 'cos you're good in bed, either!" She winked at him. "I see how far you've come, and see Johnny growing so fast, and what a happy boy he is, and I know I've had something to do with it. He's not mine, but that doesn't mean I love him any less. I'm the only mother he's ever known, anyway."

She was smiling at Johnny trying to get the spaghetti into his mouth. "Sure, one day we'll have another baby—not yet, but someday, one that's yours and mine both, but Johnny will always be special to me. You know the reason I got the 'thing' was not just to make it easier to carry him around."

Keith shook his head. "I didn't know that."

She was a bit hesitant, and was looking for his reaction when she said, "It was a little irrational maybe, because then I didn't know for sure if you'd be staying with me or not, maybe even a little sneaky, but I got it so he'd bond with me, so he'd know he was wanted and be comfortable with me. It's what my dad did with me when I was born. They didn't have those things back then, in the stores, but Dad made one, and carried me around in it almost every waking moment until I got too big. He called it an 'experiment in male nurturing' so his buddies wouldn't think he'd lost his mind, even kept some records for awhile, he said."

Keith reached over and took her hand. "I don't think it was sneaky—it was you doing what you do best. Loving."

"At first it felt strange. Every day when you left, I'd put the thing on, with him in it, and sit at the 'puter and do my work. Did a number on my back, and my hormonal balances too, I'm sure, but it worked. He was so little then, he fit right here," she indicated the space between her breasts, "and seemed like it was just where he should be. I was afraid you'd think I was being really silly, or maybe trying to show off, like hey, look what a great mother I am--so that's why I never said anything."

"You are a great mother, honey, don't ever doubt that."

"I have to admit, Clarisse used to really make me feel inadequate. But you, and Vickie and Jean have really tried hard to make me understand I shouldn't feel that way. The other day, she caught me off guard, and it all came back again. But it won't happen again, no matter what she does. She's such a sham…"

Keith got up and went around the high chair to out his arms around Mary. "You're right, there, and I know it, too. I love you, and I don't want you to ever doubt that, either."

"Oh, I don't—not anymore."

The baby started to fuss, and Keith said, "Well, which do you want, baby or dishes?"

"Guess I'll take baby this time." She gave him a quick kiss on the cheek, and reached for the baby. "Hey, I've got a question for you now."

"What's that?"

"How come you always laugh when I tell you my little fantasies?" It had been an afternoon of fantasies fulfilled.

Keith's response was a broad smile. "You really want to know?"

"Yes, I do, tell me!"

"It's because they're all so blessedly normal." He chuckled and began clearing the table.

CHAPTER FOURTEEN

People talk a lot about what they would do if a certain situation occurred. They say, "Sure I'll do the right thing," as if they mean it, and maybe they do at that moment, but when the situation actually comes up, they do something entirely different. Keith Astor was a fallible human being, like any other, so when Clarisse showed up at the apartment one day in tears, looking fragile and bereft, he let her in. It was raining, and by now it was full winter in the Pacific Northwest, so it was cold as well.

At least three people had told him this was something he should never do, but Mary wasn't home that morning—she was at the pediatrician's with Johnny, so he thought five minutes couldn't hurt.

When Mary came back an hour early, she could identify the smell the minute she came in the door. She hesitated a moment, and took a deep breath before following the smell to the kitchen. She told herself, "This one's going my way," and kissed the sleeping baby on the top of the head.

Clarisse was sitting at the table, a crumpled piece of paper in her hand. She was wearing the same pale blue raincoat she had been wearing the day she hurt Johnny, but now it was grubby and stained. Her hair, which had once been a perfect metallic vision of gold, looked overbleached, thin, and wiry. It was much shorter than it used to be—the hair extensions had fallen out long ago. One or two of her long, fake fingernails had been torn off, and she hadn't bothered replacing them. Mary wondered how long it had been since she had a bath.

Ignoring Clarisse, she went over to Keith, sitting at the other end of the table, as if it was a perfectly ordinary occurrence to have a blond crone at her kitchen table. Keith took the baby out of the 'thing', as he normally would, and raised his face for a kiss. "You're early," he remarked. Hearing Daddy's voice, the baby stirred, but he'd had a big morning, and went back to sleep.

"Doc had an emergency; we rescheduled," she murmured, as she gave him a lengthy, soulful kiss as if she'd been on a six-month safari to Zimbabwe. One hand reached up under his sweater, stroking his chest—or at least the part she could reach around the baby. He wasn't quite sure what she was up to, but didn't protest. She came up for air, and said, "Oh, hi, Clarisse, I see you got your mail today, too!"

"Mail?" asked Keith, puzzled.

Mary produced the letter from the district court out of a coat pocket. "It's final, I didn't open it, but we all know what it is, don't we?" She smiled at Clarisse, a steel, sharpened-edge smile. "This means we are finally legally free from this poor excuse for a human being."

Keith opened the letter, and grinned. "So that's it," he said, looking at Clarisse. He didn't say anything else. He watched her closely for her next move.

Clarisse tried hard to look like the inured party. In her little-girl voice, she said, "I thought maybe if I let you have some playtime with this little slut, you'd get it out of your system and come back where you belonged. Let her keep the baby, if that's what she wants. I don't want it, all I want is you, Keefie sweets! I promise, I've changed. I've been to rehab—I'll get the tits fixed, if that's what you want…they'll be so big and so hot you could smother--"

She was interrupted by Mary, who said calmly, "Clarisse, the reason Keith and Johnny came to me is because they had to, to get away from you. You want Keith, that's all. I notice you didn't say anything about love, because you don't understand what it is. Keith lives with me because he chooses to. I don't have him, or own him. I love him."

As she was removing the 'thing', taking off her coat, Mary turned to Keith and said, "I know something you don't know. When we left the doc's we stopped at Vic's to say hello. And guess who was there, Brother Kevin, that's who. Your dear brother who didn't see any harm in telling her where we lived, and where we did our grocery shopping on Tuesday mornings. Mom thought he was being concerned when he was asking all those questions about us."

Keith was stunned. "It was Kevin?" He looked over at Clarisse, disgusted.
Clarisse didn't know what to do. Nobody was yelling. Maybe Mary's calm manner confused her. At any rate, she was silent, looking at Mary with curiosity.

Mary put the thing on the table, and draped her coat over the back of the chair, casually pulled out the chair and sat down at the table. "Seems he and Clarisse had a little get-together last night. They've been an item for a while, you know what she does. She's been up to her old tricks, so they both got arrested. Drunk driving, and something else. She's not careful anymore, he's got bad scratches all over his face from those fingernails. He's worried about his job—isn't that a hoot?" She wasn't laughing. She leaned forward, and spoke directly to Clarisse. "That's an example of how you've changed, huh? Get the fuck out of my house." She reached into her coat pocket behind her for the cellular, and handed it to Keith. "Would you call Vic, honey?" She stood and pushed the chair back in, with such force it shook the table.

Clarisse stood up, desperately trying to match Mary's cool demeanor. "How can you do this to me, Keefie sweets? You know how much I love you—I can't live without you. I-I'll kill myself!" she was fumbling in her pockets. Unsteady and hung over, she was rapidly losing control.

"Go ahead." Keith said, his eyes cold. He began dialing the phone.

"They took it away from you last night, Clarisse. Illegal weapons, that was the other charge." Mary said to Keith, while picking up the 'thing', and holding it in both hands, apparently absentmindedly, flipping the straps back and forth.

There wasn't a thing Keith could do. With the baby in one arm, the phone in his other hand, he could only watch as Clarisse lost any last shred of control she may have had.

Clarisse was gasping, crying for real. Frustrated, agitated, she lunged for Mary with her broken talons. Mary held the 'thing' in front of her, catching Clarisse's claws in the straps, and pushed, as hard as she could. It was enough to knock Clarisse off balance, and she fell backward against the doorway, hitting her head. She slumped to the floor, sobbing, defeated.

"I told you to get the fuck out of my house. Response time is now about 2 minutes, so you better run," Mary leaned down and said. "And by the way, I used to go out with Kevin myself. How does it feel picking up my leftovers?"

Calling Mary every name she could think of, Clarisse scrambled to her feet, her breathing heavy, and made her way to the front door, bouncing off walls as she went. "I'll show you, bitch!" she shrieked before she slammed the door, waking the baby.

Mary sat down at the table, putting her head in her hands. "Another thirty seconds, I would've lost it," she whispered, finally allowing herself to be frightened. She looked up at Keith. "Did I handle that wrong? Are you mad at me now?"

"He's wet, I'll get him," Keith said, setting the phone on the table. "Two   minutes?" He was actually close to laughing in amazement. He'd never seen anyone shut down Clarisse so efficiently before.

"I made that up, sounded good at the time. Who'd you call, anyway?"

"I called myself—left the other phone in the car. Too bad Vickie wasn't here to see that. No honey, I am not mad at you." He dropped a kiss on the top of her head, and took the baby in for a change. "Mommy's growin' balls, son, we better watch that," he said to Johnny, loud enough so Mary could hear.

CHAPTER FIFTEEN

"I wish this could have been different," he said, looking out the kitchen window out onto the parking lot. He was speaking to Mary as she came from the bedroom.

"Different how, Bro?" Her mind was on the wedding that evening, the baby in her arms, a zillion things. Johnny was a year old, and getting heavy to hold these days. He was trying to pull her earrings off, while simultaneously trying to get down on the rug and play. Mary gave in, and gently set him down on the hall rug.

"I wish Kevin could be here, for one thing." Kevin had been off the family radar for months. He'd skipped Christmas at the senior Astors', as Keith had done the year before.

"He might show up, yet. Phil and Brian went over to gang up on him. He knows you're ready to bury the hatchet. He's just feeling terribly guilty, you know. Things could have been so much worse…"

She was interrupted by the ringing of the doorbell.

"Oh, I'll bet that's Mom and Dad!" Mary went to the door to greet her parents, Bob and Diane Stephenson. Keith picked up Johnny and followed behind.

"Whoa! They grow em tall here, or what, Mary!" her dad exclaimed when he saw Keith.

Bob was only 5'7" and bulky…nearly an exact opposite of Keith's slenderness.

"Must be the air, or something," she said. "But he's a man who can stand up to a baby, Dad! Look! Now, is that balls or what?"

"Far-fucking-out! Look at that, Diane." Bob looked up at Keith with appreciation and respect. "Sir, let me shake your hand."

Keith grinned at Mary in surprise, and shrugged. Shifting John to one arm, he reached out the other hand to Mary's dad. "Dr. Stephenson."

"Sir. Do you love her?" Bob's gaze met Keith's and held. He honestly wanted to know.

Keith was every bit as unwavering. "Without reservation," he said seriously.

"Hey, it's Dad, Mr. Tall Guy." He took Keith's big hand in both of his in some sort of serious guy shake.

"You can't remember a name for a second, can you, Bob?" Diane asked, in a loving tone.

Keith smiled at this woman who was exactly like Mary would be in 18 years. She could well be mistaken for an older sister. She was, in fact, only a few years older than brother Phil. He was glad to see her.

"I can usually make five minutes. Keith Astor, you have made a woman out of my little girl. You have my undying respect. Please—marry her, give her babies. This is what she has always wanted." Bob Stephenson was sniffling, his eyes full of tears.

Keith didn't know what to say to that. Couldn't say anything, anyway, because Dad reached out his arms and enfolded him, the baby and Mary in a bear hug. "Basics, man—it's what it's all about."

Then he wanted to hold the baby, since he hadn't held a child since Mary. "You know, I'd swear this was Mary's child, he looks just like her."

Keith said, "I keep telling her that, and she doesn't believe me. You know, she did that bonding thing with the carrier, just like you did, Dad, I wonder if that has anything to do with it—you know, nature vs. nurture?" Perhaps it was deliberate, but Keith had chosen Bob Stephenson's favorite subject. He had plenty to say, and didn't hesitate to fill Keith in.

Meanwhile, Mary was showing her mother the photos of both families on the wall. These weren't the same pictures Keith had before in his apartment, or even copies, but Keith said they were better. Mary had spent a long time getting pictures from Jean and all the brothers, then enlarging and framing, even going so far as to drag Keith to a portrait studio. Every single Astor and Stephenson was on the display that covered almost the whole wall. Mary hoped, in some small way, it would make up for the loss of the old pictures and provide a positive memory to overshadow a bad one.

Diane was saying, "Ooh!' in the same tone Keith had heard Mary use before, only not in the living room, talking to somebody other than him.

Keith left Bob telling Johnny all about the psychological dynamics of blended families in the dining room, and saw Diane was looking at the picture of brother Phil on Kirk's boat. Even Keith had to admit the old fart was lookin' good in that one. He had a tan like Keith used to have, and was in excellent shape from working outside all the time. He'd brought his son Derek's swimming trunks by mistake, at least two sizes too small, but wore them anyway.

"Don't even think about it, Mom, you're in Monogamy Central here, and I'm not kidding! Strictly enforced by four very large, determined women. Soon to be five." Mary was saying. "I'm not as tall as they are, well, Jean's my size, but she's the mom."

"A woman can dream, can't she?" Diane wailed, laughing.

"Sure, just keep your hands to yourself. I know what a horny old bitch you can be, Dad told me all about Guillermo last summer. These guys aren't like that, Mom, so behave yourself, huh?"

Keith was surprised to see such strong words ending with a hug. As he walked into the living room, mother and daughter were almost dancing through their first contact in years. Mary looked over Diane's shoulder and said, "Ma had the hots for Phil, but I talked her out of it!"

"Phil???" Keith gasped. "Oh, no, don't even..." He had to sit down, he was laughing so hard. "Bobbie..."

"Yeah, Bobbie—" Mary pointed her out in the photos. The picture had been taken at Jean's birthday party, when Bobbie, in her long, black, bejeweled dress, was looking like the "Empress of Astor".

Diane gulped. "Oh, my..." she said.

"Yes Mother, monogamy. What a concept! It hasn't failed here, by any stretch of the imagination." She laughed at her mother's confusion. "Don't worry, though, Keith won't tell, will he, Bro?"

"Your secret is safe with me, Diane," Keith said. He wondered for a moment how Bob could so easily allow this luminous, mature version of his own Mary to be touched and kissed by other men.

Strangers. It was bad enough when he thought Mary was being loved by his own brother. And how could Bob leave Diane, himself, for even a minute, to waste his time on someone else? But Mary was special—she didn't want anybody but him. Keith was glad Mary had chosen her own way.

"Mary, is that you!" Diane was exclaiming. For almost lost among the group of 40 or more photos of the families, there was a black-and-white, 8X10 of Keith and Mary, in which they appeared naked from the waist up. They were facing the camera, laughing. Keith was standing behind Mary, his right arm and hand gently covering Mary's breasts. It was so tastefully done, there was no hint of erotica. The effect was casual, charming—almost as if they'd been caught in the instant right after sharing a joke belonging only to them.

"That's my favorite picture, up here anyway." Keith said. "Isn't she beautiful?" He couldn't help putting both his arms around Mary, hugging her in an unconscious duplication of the photo.

"I had to stand on a box to make it work," Mary chuckled. "Jean calls it 'arty'—I don't think she really likes it much."

"You always were Miss Modesty—my how times have changed!" Bob said as he came in the living room. He looked at the photo, and grinned. "Quite lovely, no doubt about that. Always knew she'd be a beauty. You only have to look at her mother to see that."

"Is it OK if I show your mom and dad the others?" Keith asked.

"Why not—just make sure you put them away before anybody else shows up!"

Keith went over to the bookcase to get out a photo album.

Mary remembered the photo shoot well, because it had been so much fun after she relaxed a little. Keith had the idea that if they were recording images for posterity, then he wanted her breasts recorded. They were perfect right now, he said, and when they (meaning himself and Mary) were both old and flabby, he wanted to look at the pictures and remember. It wasn't like she was totally undressed, she and Keith were both wearing black pants, and most of the shots showed only a portion of a breast, maybe, using Keith's arms for cover. There were two that were especially memorable.

One showed Keith with one arm around her waist, and the other lightly resting on a breast, bending his head down, as if to catch something Mary was saying as she faced the camera, but had turned her head for an instant. They were completely involved in each other, and had actually forgotten the camera was there. Keith thought it looked like a perfume ad, but Mary loved it.

The other was an extreme close-up taken from the side of one breast, showing Keith's parted lips about an inch away.

This one had involved much discussion over which one was 'the best', and what was Keith's best side. By the time they finally decided, Mary was laughing so hard she could hardly hold her arms up out of the way.

Then it degenerated from there.

They assumed the position, and the photographer said, "It's kinda flat—perk it up a little, Keith." That set off another round of giggles, each of them swearing they wouldn't look at the other, but they couldn't help it. The photographer was laughing herself, but eventually both Keith and Mary took a deep breath, settled down, and created the moment. This was Keith's favorite. The photo could easily have been near-porn, but it wasn't. The effect was powerful magic. In light and shadow, it said something that couldn't be expressed in words about Keith's love and devotion for Mary.

"We didn't put these on the wall. My mother had a fit when she saw that one--," he said, pointing over to the wall. He handed the album to Diane, and Bob looked over her shoulder.

"Well, I don't really want to look at my boobs all the time, either," Mary chuckled.

Diane and Bob were paging through the album, and Diane said sighing, "I used to be in good shape like that, once upon a time…"

"You certainly did—still are in my opinion," Bob said. "Whew! Our little girl's got quite a set on her, huh?"

Mary and Keith looked at each other, startled, and started to chuckle.

As if he hadn't said anything at all, Bob said, "Mary, this young man is requesting a new diaper. Where might I find such an object?"

Mary, still laughing, took her dad's arm and led him into the baby's room, leaving Keith with Diane.

"I know, Keith, I'm not much of a mother figure, am I!" she began, sitting in a chair on the other side of the room. "But the way I look at it, at least I made sure she was always taken care of. For some reason, I feel the need to explain myself to you."

She dropped her shoes off onto the floor, folded her legs under her in the chair in Mary's way. "I tried to raise her to be a flag-waving, bra-burning feminist like I wanted to be, but somehow it didn't take. She was, in most aspects, raised by Mother and Bob and his friends. She loves men in a way I just don't understand. She's embraced everything I rejected. Bob thinks this is normal." She shrugged. "Who's to say?"

Diane looked around, at the photos on the wall, and her own family's antiques in the dining room. "She's into some kind of a 'roots' thing that I never felt the need for. I've always known where I came from, back for centuries. So who cares, anymore? But she's got the family silver, and that silly sideboard, and if that makes her happy…"

"She told me you wanted her to be a scientist," Keith said, sitting on the couch.

"H'm, I suppose I did, early on. But I think that was more a projection of my own frustrated desires. In the final analysis, it's whether she's fulfilled by her life's choices, not mine. I can't pretend to understand computers and technology, but she appears to enjoy it. And you're certainly not one of those deathly dull computer geeks she used to hang out with…" Diane smiled to herself, not sharing the joke.

Keith was about to ask, when Mary called from the other room, "I'll get that!"
He hadn't heard the doorbell.

Phil and Brian were at the door, both looking apologetic. Their mission of tracking down Kevin had failed.

"Nobody home at his place, and they said he hasn't shown up at work in like a week," Brian said, shrugging. "Guess it was Ma's idea, anyway. I wasn't sure it would work, even if we did find him."

"Well, at least you tried. C'mon in guys," Mary gestured behind her, and they followed her into the living room. "The big guys are here!" she announced to Keith and Diane, and with a stern look at her mom, went quickly into the other room, to get her dad. Mary had a hunch her mother would be absolutely unhinged by the Astor brothers, who did tend to fill up a room, and needed her dad to provide a dose of reality.

When she returned with Bob Stephenson, Keith was saying, "That's really not like Kev to just not show up at work—"

She caught his eye, the question unspoken in the air between them. Clarisse?
Mary prayed not. Even Kevin, as badly as he'd treated them, did not deserve her.

Bob was introducing himself, and the subject was lost in a flurry of introductions and exclamations over how big the baby was getting. Phil and Brian arrived from AZ late the night before, and hadn't seen him yet. They were surprised by this Doctor of Psychology who was so comfortable holding a baby, and by Mary's mother, who seemed far less interested in her grandchild than in them.

Mary offered coffee, and went to the kitchen to make it, followed by Keith, who was looking thoughtful. "I don't know what to think," he said, leaning back against the counter and folding his arms.

From the living room came the sound of laughter, the low voices of Keith's brothers topped by Diane's light giggles. "Mother's being engaging," Mary remarked dryly.

"She's something, now I know where you get it from," Keith said, grinning, deliberately watching Mary's reaction. "Queen Mary is not amused?"

"I don't flirt," Mary said firmly, pouring water in the coffee maker.

"Sure you do, all the time—with me."

"You, but that's different. Also depends on your definition."

"Seems pretty harmless to me, anyway. Phil and Brian are grownups, you know."

"Oh, I know, honey, it's just me, I guess."

"You've got more important things to think about right now—do you realize you're getting married in five hours?"

"I can hardly think about anything else. I'm actually nervous, can you believe that?" She looked up at Keith with rueful grin.

He put his arms around her. "You're not afraid once the ring's on your finger, I'll turn into a monster or something, are you?" He was only half kidding.

"No, it's not that, it's just the actual thing. What if I say the wrong thing, or start giggling and can't stop—or, or, I don't know."

"Well, try this—keep in mind the real reason for all of this today—so you can use Grandma's linen napkins anytime you want!"

"So, you think that's it huh?" She was laughing softly, and Keith was laughing too. He bent down to kiss her, and was interrupted by Phil.

"All right you two, save it for tonight!" he chuckled, pulling out a kitchen chair. "Wow, Mary, that mother of yours is something."

"Don't I know it," Mary muttered.

"Wrong thing to say, Phil," Keith said. "Just got her calmed down."

"Sorry about that. How's that coffee doing?" Phil said, in an attempt to change the subject. "Uh, did you mean for Diane to be showing that album around? Or is that also a touchy subject?" He was grinning, and staring directly at Mary's breasts. "Perfect, huh? Or is that just her motherly opinion? Seem a little small to me. Bobbie had more than that when she was twelve." Phil was laughing, not unkindly.

"Oh, my God, Mother…" Mary covered her face with her hands and leaned on the counter.

Keith was laughing, too. "I happen to think they are perfect. I wanted them recorded for posterity."

"So what are we gonna do now, have a vote? Put 'em up on a website, why dontcha?" Mary was recovering some of her good humor.

"Hey, there ya go," Keith said.

The doorbell rang again while Keith was quietly explaining the Stephenson's 'open marriage' to Phil. Phil thought the whole concept was hilarious.

CHAPTER SIXTEEN

Mary went again to answer the door, but this time found, to her surprise, Kevin, in a ghostly reminder of the way Keith had looked himself a year before. He hadn't shaved in a long time, the T-shirt he was wearing was ripped and stained, the jeans he was wearing could probably stand in the corner by themselves, and he was barefoot.

"Kev, what's up?" she asked.

"God, Mary, I'm sorry. Clarisse—she's got a gun." Breathing heavily from running up the stairs, he looked at Mary with that stunned, dull expression that told Mary he was using every bit of energy he had right now.

"Come on in here, Kev," she said, as she whisked him past the door to the living room and into the kitchen.

He was surprised to see Phil. "What are you doing here?"

"The wedding's tonight—what are you doing here?" Phil was just as surprised to see Kevin.

"Wedding? What wedding?" Kevin looked around, confused.

"We sent you an invitation," Keith said. "A couple of weeks ago."

"Shit, she probably got the mail. She does that sometimes and throws it all in the garbage." Kevin sank into a chair.

"Clarisse?" Keith almost didn't have to ask. Kevin nodded. "I'm so fucking sorry, Keith. I didn't know. She's been getting all dressed up for somethin' for hours. She spent like $1800 on a dress and some other stuff the other day, all on my credit card. I thought she'd be on her way here, she kept talkin' about she was gonna show that slut, and mumblin' some shit, sounded like Keefie sweets—isn't that what she used to call you? Where's the wedding at?"

"It's at Dad's." Keith and Phil looked at each other, and Keith grabbed for the phone. "Is Vickie home?" he asked Phil.

Phil shrugged. "Try her pager," he said, and looked at Kevin, appalled. "You never learn do you?" he said to Kevin, and went to get Brian.

"I haven't seen her this bad in a long time. She was OK, for a long time. After the divorce was final, it was like she got used to it...anyway, she's really wasted, on what, I don't know..."

"Well, you look like shit," Brian said, taking Phil's chair. "Where've you been?" He wasn't any happier to see him than Phil was.

Brian was preparing to give Kevin a piece of his mind, when Keith looked at him and said in a low voice, "Don't—he's had enough."

Neither Brian nor Phil was used to the youngest giving them orders, and that's what it was. They kept silent.

Keith said, "I got Vickie—they're at Dad's already. Not a damn thing we can do now."

Mary left Keith talking to Kevin, quietly, with the other two brothers looking on, dumfounded. After months of bad blood and outright hatred between the two youngest Astors, they didn't know what to make of this sudden change of heart.

Mary went to try to explain to her parents what was happening. She hadn't said much to them about Keith's ex-wife, thinking the less said the better. Her dad hadn't practiced in years, and she had no idea what his take on the situation would be.

She dreaded having to listen to his long-winded pronouncement of everybody's innermost thoughts.

They had been lulled into a sense of security by months of living normally, with no idea that Kevin would be the catalyst that brought it all up. Again, though, she was not afraid of anything Clarisse would do or try to do. She was angry to see her wedding day ruined by a woman who should've been in jail, who always seemed to elude having to take responsibility for her actions. She wondered if there were other men, other families who been victimized by Clarisse. How long would this all go on?

Her dad was sitting on the floor, playing with Johnny, her mother watching him with a puzzled expression. "What's happening?" Diane asked.

Mary gave them a bare-bones account of the past year, trying to present it in as detached a fashion as possible, mainly explaining why Kevin had arrived out of the blue. When Bob started his expected barrage of questions, she held up her hands and said, "Later, Dad. Not now. Just keep an eye on Johnny for awhile, alright?"

She went back into the kitchen, where Keith, Brian and Phil were trying to make some sense if it all. Kevin was missing. "Where'd he go?" she asked.

Keith shrugged. "I didn't know what to do with him, so I sent him to the shower. Not getting much out of him. Besides, he smelled like Clarisse, and I couldn't stand it. At least I got a shower once in a while." He tried to smile.

"His bathroom door doesn't lock." Mary looked at Keith, and a knowing passed between them. To the others she explained, "He's probably been sleeping in his clothes for a week. And you're not going to get anything out of him, not just yet. This isn't over."

She sighed, and rested her hands on Keith's shoulders. "I'm not letting her mess up our wedding, Bro. It's not going to happen."

There was silence in the room. They could hear the shower running, and Bob and Johnny having what amounted to a conversation in the living room. Phil looked at Mary, puzzled. "You think he actually understands what the baby's saying?"

Mary smiled in spite of herself, and just as she began to form a reply, something banged into the kitchen window—a plastic soda bottle, empty. Then they heard the unmistakable sound of Clarisse, through the wall. The sound of it made Mary shudder, as she remembered how it had been before. This time there weren't any headphones to block the noise, and this time it was her problem, as well as Keith's.

Without a word to anyone, she turned and went to the front door. She opened it and stood on the top step by the landing. Keith, Brian and Phil were right behind her, all saying "Mary! What are you doing!" more or less simultaneously. She ignored them, and looked down at Clarisse.

Clarisse was dressed for a wedding, in a short, ice-blue chiffon suit. It was tasteful, elegant—or would have been had the blouse underneath it not been see-through net. The blouse was tight over her big, implanted breasts and the material flattened and distorted their shape. She was even wearing a hat on her now medium-length blond hair. A hat with a veil, like the kind seen on guests at televised royal weddings. Leave it to

Clarisse to copy something she saw on television, Mary thought wryly. Instead of a purse in her right hand, she was carrying a gun. Ironically, it was a lot like the .38 she and Keith had fought over, but Mary couldn't tell whether it was loaded or not. Behind her was a white Cadillac, no doubt her father's. Both doors were open, and the engine was still running.

"Kevvybaby, you sonofabitch, what are you doing here? You told, you fucking bastard!" Mary looked behind her, and there between Brian and Phil, was Kevin in a towel.

"Clarisse—" he started to say.
"There's no talking to her now, Kev, you know that," said Keith, standing behind Mary, gripping her shoulders so hard it almost hurt.

"Brainless fuck, you good-for-nothing, Kevvy! All I want is my Keefie sweets! Wanna get rid of the slut, I can have my Keefie sweets!" Clarisse was nearly incoherent. She was staggering against the door of the car, holding on with one hand to keep from falling over.

Behind her, the police arrived, apparently called by Vickie and behind them, Vickie and Kirk. Clarisse turned to look at them, without surprise as if she knew they were coming. "Hope you're still laughing now, Keith!" she bellowed. She lifted the gun, pointed it at her temple, and fired. Missing, she staggered, slightly wounded, fired again. This time the bullet hit its mark, and the other side of her head exploded, taking the hat and splatters of tissue and blood across the hood of the car. Her body collapsed, landing between the open door and the frame. What was left of her face stared at the group of Astors on the stairs.

As the officers approached carefully, guns drawn, Kevin moved to go downstairs. Brian and Phil each grabbed an arm, preventing him from moving. "Nobody's going anywhere," said Phil, the biggest brother, in charge again.

Mary turned around and buried her face in Keith's shirt.

Vickie and Kirk came running around the police car, as soon as the officers holstered their weapons and approached Clarisse, now without a doubt, dead. "Mary, you are an idiot," said Vickie, as angry as she'd ever been.

Mary raised her head from Keith's chest and not looking at Vickie, said, "I know, you think I could've been hurt. Don't ask me how I know, but I was sure that's what she was going to do. "People like that remind me of Windows95--looks good on the surface but you just know there's a General Protection Fault waiting to happen in there somewhere." She was looking behind Keith and caught a glimpse of her mother inside, staring at Kevin. Oops. "Kev, you lost your towel," she said, casually, surprising even herself.

Maybe later she would react, but right now they had a wedding to go to. Hers and Keith's. Finally.

CHAPTER SEVENTEEN

There were a lot of questions to be answered, and soon there were more police, an ambulance, sirens blaring, and a crowd of curious neighbors outside taking in the ghastly scene. It took hours for the confusion to settle down. Mary and Keith were both glad they were moving soon.

Knowing it was all over made it feel a bit less intrusive as they began to dress for their wedding. The Stephensons went back to their hotel to change, and Phil and Brian, along with Vickie and Kirk, headed over to the senior Astors to change as well. The original plan had been for Keith to go back to his dad's with his brothers, and Mary to go over with her parents, but now there wasn't time for superstitious nonsense. Besides, Mary didn't want to let Keith or Kevin out of her sight.

Even though he felt like hell and was in no mood, Mary persuaded Kevin to come to the wedding. Keith really wanted him there, she explained. They needed to be a family again more than they needed to give fuel to an old feud; especially since the source of it all had removed herself. Wearing Keith's grey suit that Mary had loved so much when Keith was wearing it, after a shower and shave, even Keith agreed Kev looked almost human.

Keith was stunning, of course in dark blue.

"Ooh, yum," Mary said when she saw him come into the bedroom, in the reflection in the mirror. She was adjusting the tiny silk flowers in her hair.

"Yum yourself, you are gorgeous, my love. I'm afraid to touch you, you look so pristine—dare I say, virginal?" Keith put his hands lightly on her shoulders and brushed her forehead with his lips.

She and Vickie had shopped for days to find this fitted white silk dress that was simplicity itself. "We can pretend, can't we?" she said, as Keith helped her fasten the gold chain she'd borrowed from her mother.

They went into the living room to pick up the baby and check him one last time before they all left. Johnny was going to spend a few days with Aunt Brenda and Uncle Brian in Arizona. Kevin was sitting on the couch, paging through the photo album that was quickly becoming a family anecdote, like Keith being born on the deck, or the time they were both in sixth grade and Keith did all Kevin's homework for six months before they got caught.

"The time Mary and Keith had 'those' pictures taken," Mary said softly, with a little smile to Keith. She went over to the playpen to pick up Johnny.

"You were right, Keith, they are perfect," Kevin said, closing the book and leaning back, sadly watching Mary fuss over Keith's child. "What did Mom and Dad say about that?"

"Mom was a little, uh, shocked I guess you'd say, by that one up there, so we decided not to press it." Keith said, pointing over Kevin's head to the photos on the wall.

"All those are new aren't they? What happened to the old ones?"

"Clarisse took them down from the wall at the old place, lined them up on the bed, with me in it, and shot them—one by one," Keith said, no longer upset by the incident. "Then when we moved in here, Mary called everybody and got them to send new ones for my birthday. Then, I realized she wasn't in any of them, so we got those done."

"Fucking bitch," Kevin said, with clenched teeth. "Oh! I'm sorry, Mare, not you. Clarisse—shit, she didn't want to have anything to do with the family at all." He sighed and said, "Christ, I missed you guys."

"It's like you've been away somewhere, isn't it?" Keith said.

The wedding itself was nothing like she imagined Keith's first would have been. Kevin had come to see her the next day and told her all the details he could remember, but the main point was that it was huge and showy, a bit over the top as far as Kevin was concerned.

This one was only the Astors, and the Stephensons in the senior Astor's living room. The only decoration in the room to show this was a wedding at all was a big arrangement of white roses on the mantelpiece over the huge fireplace. Mary's bouquet was small, only a few white roses tied with a ribbon. No bridesmaids, ushers, or any of that. Keith, Mary, a judge--and the ceremony itself didn't take more than fifteen minutes. Johnny slept through the entire thing in Grandpa Stephenson's arms.

Jean and Bobbie, and even Pete had tried to persuade Mary to have a bigger wedding, one that would obliterate the memory of the other one by its sheer elegance. But Mary stood firm in her resolve to be married quietly, with as little fuss as possible. As things turned out, she was right. A big wedding would have seemed crass and uncaring after the afternoon's event.

Clarisse's suicide had cast a shadow over the proceedings, but they were all also relieved that the 'bad time' was over. Time to heal. A wedding seemed a good way to begin.

Bobbie said, "The smallest wedding for the smallest wife!" as she hugged Mary when it was over.

Then of course, she 'had' to kiss all the brothers. "For the first and last time, I'm willing to bet," she whispered to her mother.

"Guess you can't blame them," Diane said wistfully.

Everybody was helping themselves to the buffet in the dining room when Mary noticed Kevin was missing. She found him out on the deck, which had a view of the mountains, even at nine o'clock on a summer evening.
He was leaning on the railing, alone.

"You OK, big guy?"

"Not really. Tired beyond belief."

"I know." She leaned on the railing next to him.

"Do you?"

"When Keith came over to my place that night, he was so tired he didn't have any idea what was happening to him. He was going to the hospital to be with Johnny every day, and after that he'd go home and deal with her. Of course she didn't want him to go to the hospital. She never saw Johnny once before Keith brought him home. I don't think he'd had any sleep for a month, and I'm not kidding."

Kevin was silent a moment. "I've been pretty fucking stupid," he said quietly, to the empty back yard.

"Not stupid, Kev, but arrogant. You thought you could deal with her. And you've paid for it. Big time." Mary said.

"I hear ya there," Keith said, coming across the deck to join them. Kevin stood up and turned around to look at his brother. A look passed between them, but neither one said anything.

She winked at him and, "Somehow they just don't have what other people have that tells them their needs aren't the most important in the world. They have to make people do what they want and somehow they don't even know that is so totally wrong." Mary looped both her arms through the guys' arms, resting on the railing, and held their hands. "Then after they've been around their kids long enough, the kids learn it, too, so it goes on and on. I just hope my dad's nurture vs. nature theory is right, and John doesn't grow up to be like his mother—his birth mother, that is."

"At least he's not a girl," Kevin said, his voice a low growl.

"And what's wrong with girls, pray tell?" Jean asked, as she came out for a minute to see what they were up to. "I think it would be lovely to have a girl in the family—at last! With five sons and five grandsons, I think it's about time Grandma had a girl to spoil. I've had a chest of pink baby clothes in the attic for so long they're practically antiques."

"And maybe if I ever have a girl, she won't be so damn tall, either—ya think, Jean?" Mary turned around, grinning at her mother-in-law.

"Yes, not only are we outnumbered, we're outsized, aren't we dear? Well, the future is in your hands, and I leave you to it!" Laughing, she patted Mary on the shoulder, and said to Kevin, "Make sure you get something to eat!" And went back inside.

Then Keith said, "Have you kissed the bride yet?"

"Better not," Kevin said, with regret. "God knows what kinda shit Clarisse mighta given me."

"Oh, don't be silly," Mary said, standing on tiptoe and kissing Kevin on the cheek.

Kevin wrapped his arms around her, pulling her close, and said to Keith, "Too bad I couldn't just borrow her sometime."

"Two chances," Mary said. "Nonexistent and none!"

"You still know how to say no loud and clear, dontcha?" Kevin chuckled, letting her go. "Were—were you OK ?" he asked Keith.

"Yeah we lucked out, me and Johnny both. And of course Mrs. Astor here never got any since college, so we didn't hafta worry about her—"

"Shut up, Keith," Mary began, embarrassed. "Anyway, Kev, I bet you don't know we're moving, do you?"

"You are? Where?"

"Arizona," Keith said. "I'm going to work for Brian."

"You don't know jack about computers."

"I do now. Took some online courses, and of course, Mary helped. So now I'm a computer teacher."

"When's this happening?"

"By September, anyway." Mary said. "Tomorrow we're going to Sedona for a few days, then down to Phoenix to look at houses. Bobbie and Brenda have picked out 5 or 6 for us to look at that aren't too far from them, in Scottsdale. Keith'll finally have his own pool!"

"You'll be all fried like Phil," Kevin observed. "Hell, that only leaves me and Kirk here—is Mom OK with it?" He remembered Jean's near-breakdown after Keith's first marriage.

"Yeah, I think so," Keith said, leaning against the railing. "But there's no way I'd get a job around here anymore, and I think she understands that. We'll be up for the birthday party and Christmas like everybody else, and maybe they can come down to Arizona for a change."

Mary could see that Kevin wasn't thrilled with the news. "We'll be around for a while, Kev."

She turned around and looked through the glass doors into the dining room. Jean was turning lights on, as the daylight was fading. The three sisters-in-law were sitting at the dining room table, and she could see beyond them into the living room, where the brothers and the grandparents were being entertained by the smallest member of the family. He had lost his birth mother today, but would never feel a sense of loss. The woman he knew as his mother was still here, and no matter if Mary had children of her own, there would always be a special place for Johnny in her heart. He had been born in the seventh ring of hell, and she prayed that he would never have to go back there again.

FINIS

Trudy W. Schuett

Friends to the End

www.ingramcontent.com/pod-product-compliance
Lightning Source LLC
Chambersburg PA
CBHW050513260626
47157CB00004B/1306